FAST GUN

Preacher caught the weapon in mid-flight and froze. Donner could draw and fire at any second, and all could claim Preacher had had a weapon in his hand. He had been set up. He was a dead patsy and he felt as sick inside as the day Charles Barrington had taught him to fast draw and then challenged him. He was looking sure death square in the face.

The freeze position, with the caught weapon in his upraised right hand lasted only a second, then he expertly tossed the lightweight gun over to his left hand. It stalled Donner's draw and caught his attention. The moment Preacher saw Donner's hands close down over the pistol hilts, he fired, spun to his right as he fanned the hammer of the piece, and fired again. Jerry Donner's hands never got the pistols out of the hilts of the sheath leather.

Also in the PREACHER'S LAW series:

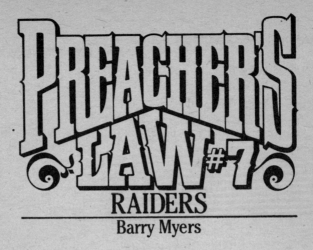

PREACHER'S LAW #7

RAIDERS

Barry Myers

LEISURE BOOKS  **NEW YORK CITY**

A LEISURE BOOK

February 1989

Published by

Dorchester Publishing Co., Inc.
276 Fifth Avenue
New York, NY 10001

Copyright © 1989 by Barry Myers

Printed in the United States of America

PREFACE

Bradburn Hill - 1908

NATHAN HALE BREED got off the evening train at Tusculum, Tennessee. He prayed he would never have to make the rail journey to Sikeston, Missouri again. A wire awaited him from Ned Buntline in New York.

CEASE THIS FOOLISH TRAVEL STOP HAVE EVIDENCE OF WOMAN WHO OBTAINED PREACHER'S BANK VAULT RECORDS STOP YOU ARE ON TRAIL OF HOAX STOP NED.

The dime novel author grinned. It was the first bit of fact his fiction writing co-author had ever given him on their combined work of "The Life and Times of a Gunslinger—James David Preacher."

Nate Breed believed in his heart that Preacher was still alive. Buntline wanted him to stay dead, lost in the bay during the San Francisco earthquake. Dead, the novel was making them a small fortune, even though great portions of the book were based on pure fiction right out of Buntline's head. Alive, the man who had become known as The Widow Maker would force the true facts to be printed, just as his distant kin were demanding.

Nate Breed wanted the truth, no matter the outcome. Had there been no earthquake, his years of research on the man would not have been burned in the hotel fire. Had there been no earthquake, he would not have lost the key to the safety deposit box when he was dumped into the bay mud. But, there had been an earthquake, a fictional book that embarrassed him, a scathing letter on the book which brought him from New York to Tennessee, a rush trip to Preacher's old stomping grounds of Sikeston, and now back again to this lonely depot in Tennessee.

The telegraph encouraged him, rather than discouraged him. He believed he was closing in on the truth with a reporter's zeal. He tucked it away and asked directions to the Tusculum livery stable.

Fifteen minutes later, Breed was chuckling to himself. The horse had balked at having his wicker suitcase tied behind the saddle and he had to repack everything in a rented saddlebag. It brought back vivid memories. In his younger days, when he roamed the west cutting Preacher's trail, he had sat several hundred hired livery horses and learned to live out of a saddlebag. This hired nag acted as though she had carried nothing but Confederate soldiers and resented the smell of having a Yankee on her back. The mare learned quickly who was boss.

Nate grasped the reins firmly and pulled the horse's head to the left. "No, you bag of bones, we do not want to go into Bradburn Hill. I want this left hand road, which should take me to the Barrett Plantation. I wish you could tell me if the former slave, Luke Barrett, is still alive. I don't trust asking anyone around here such a direct question. They just might send me off on another wild goose chase."

For several miles each side of the dusty road was lined with small farms, weather grayed clapboard cabins and family groups working their acre or two of land. The war had been over for 43 years and there were still few signs of recovery. The white farmers eyed him with caution and the children hid behind the full skirts of their mothers. The black farmers pretended to ignore him but their children eyed him with open curiosity. The only strangers seen on that road were tax collectors.

Then something caught his eye that made him pull the horse up short. A brightly painted blue and white sign hung over the gate entry to a farm which was in stark contrast to the others. Here the neat rows stretched to the next horizon, the cotton bolls making the landscape look like bushes of white roses. The main house and farm buildings were sparkling white and the gardens well tended. Only one person was in sight, a serving girl clearing away dishes from a large table on the veranda. The rest of the farm was held in lazy, hazy, late afternoon heat waves. From what he had just been viewing, it was like a desert mirage.

"Bradburn Hill Farm," he mused, reading the sign. "Of course! It is only natural that his kin would have kept the name of the old Preacher plantation alive."

A giggle took him by surprise. He looked down to see a girl of about twelve step from behind a gooseberry bush with a near full basket. Her hair was tied up in a hundred little pigtails and her face showed that she had been sampling her task. She came to the horse with no outward show of fear.

"Weren't no Preacher kin who named de farm, mistah. Dat's de name my great-gran-pappy gave ta it.'"

"I didn't realize I had spoken aloud," Nate said, politely taking off his hat. "Whom do I have the honor of addressing?"

There was no shy giggle, but a respectful curtsey. "I am named Pansy Barrett, suh."

"I'm very pleased to meet you, Miss Pansy. I am Nathan Hale Breed. Barrett? I would take it that your great-grandfather is Luke Barrett."

"That he is, suh." She produced a grin of even whiter teeth. "Would you be knowing him?"

Nate nodded. Once, in Tombstone, Arizona, over Teton Jack, Preacher had listed the men he most admired in life. His father, Morgan Lake, Nathan Bedford Forrest, but heading the list was Luke Barrett, the illegitimate son of Denning Barrett and the man sent West with Preacher when he had been banished from home.

"I've heard many stories about him and look forward to meeting him."

The girl frowned. "Oh, suh, you am mighty late to be arrivin' for granpappy Luke's dinner party. It was a real nice affair, too."

Nate grinned. "I really wasn't invited, Miss Pansy. Were there a lot of interesting people?" Nate tried to keep his voice calm.

He was greeted with a shrug and an even broader grin of white teeth. "Only white folk I knew was Auntie Morgana. Dat would be her carriage goin' up ta main plantation road."

"Are the other guests still with your great-grandfather?"

"No, suh!" She giggled again. "And my gramma-lady done put gran-pappy Luke to bed, 'cause she says he had too much of that Teton Jack to drink with the tall man."

Nate Breed's heart pounded so wildly in his chest that he could feel the beats in his temple. He was well aware of one tall man who had a passion for drinking Teton Jack—Preacher! He knew he had pushed Miss Pansy to the limit of her knowledge, but she had given him a wealth of other information.

All the way back from Sikeston he had questioned whether JenaBelle Trotter had given him truth or more fiction. "Auntie Morgana" underlined that it was truth. His puzzlement was her carriage heading for the Barrett Plantation. JenaBelle claimed that Morgana Lake had married Preacher's brother Zachary. But, she was alive and close at hand. A woman who knew more about Preacher than any woman alive.

"Miss Pansy, I'm going to ride ahead and pay my respects to Miss Morgana. If your memory is good, tell your gran-pappy Luke I would like to return and pay my respects to him."

"Dey say I'se too smart fur my britches, Mr. Nathan Hale Breed. I'll not be forgetting."

Nate rode away chuckling. He was sure she would be a very exact messenger. But not the black coachman, when he caught up with the carriage. The man refused to pull the carriage to a stop and eyed Breed as though he were a highwayman. Only a command from the lone occupant, hidden behind a parasol and veiled hat, finally got him to pull to a stop, but with the whip at the ready to use either on Breed or the horses.

Nate took off his hat and looked down into the open carriage. "I believe I have the honor and pleasure of addressing Morgana Lake. Excuse me, Mrs. Zachaty Preacher."

The black coachman turned on him a scathing look that

would have made any other man flinch. "Suh, you are addressing the Widow Barrett, the wife of our late Mas'sa Brent Barrett. Southern gentlemen don't address a lady or a widow, 'cept through another lady and not 'for dey be giving us a name!"

Morgana Lake Barrett closed the parasol and pushed back the veil. She looked up at Breed with a wry smile. "You must forgive Moses, sir. His father, Juice Harp, was a coachman for the Preacher family for many years. Southern coachmen are traditionalists when it comes to protecting their womanfolk. Moses, this gentleman is Nathan Hale Breed and would have no knowledge that I have recently buried my husband of thirty-five years, Colonel Brent Barrett. Nor was I aware, until this moment, that Mr. Breed had returned from his trip to Missouri."

"You were aware of my first visit here?"

Morgana laughed. It still held the magical alto ring of her youth. Although in her early seventies, Nate Breed could still see youth in the thin; triangular face, with the slightly pugged nose, wide mouth and still captivating smile. The spring carrot hair was softened by silver, but the snapping green eyes were alive and devilish.

"We are still a little world here, Mr. Breed. As I was still in mourning, it was not proper to accept gentlemen callers. This afternoon was my first time out in public. It was nice to spend it with friends—dear old friends."

"Especially those who like to drink Teton Jack?" he asked, a little too pointedly.

"Some of us have been partial to that libation for some time, sir."

"You know exactly what I mean and why I am here. I seek the truth about Preacher!"

"Truth?" she scoffed. "I found very little truth about the man in that tasteless bit of fiction that you and Mr. Buntline wrote. It was a horrible piece of garbage."

It was Nate's turn to smile. "So you so expertly pointed out in your letter to Ned Buntline and myself." He paused, waiting for her to deny that charge.

When she did not, he went on with a note of encouragement. "I do not deny that the book is filled with fiction. Had my research notes survived the earthquake, or had I not lost the key to Preacher's safety deposit box, it might have been written quite differently. Even though Mr. Buntline sees no merit in rewriting the book, I seek truth for my own piece of mind. You must keep in mind that in all the years I knew the man, he would only give me bits and pieces of his life.''

Morgana nodded and sat up straight in the carriage seat. Although a petite woman, the posture made her seem taller and formidable.

"Peace of mind," she said softly. "You knew him, and yet I could not find him in that book. Your quest was for sensational blood and gore. He was my friend and brother. He was unique among men."

"Was?" Breed gasped. "You are the first person, in my odyssey for truth, who has dared use the past tense. I question that strongly. Miss Pansy Barrett told me you all sat and drank Teton Jack with a tall man."

Morgana looked trapped for a moment and then grinned. "They would all be tall men to Pansy, and they are all delighted to sip Teton Jack. Don't use Pansy as an authority, sir. Her father thought he could make a better living in the North and they have been back home only a couple of months. She knows very few of the county people on sight."

"I was using you as my authority," he said, then regretted its snappish tone. "Your words suggested he was dead, and it startled me."

"Some men never die, Mr. Breed. Their body, yes; but their spirit, never. I used the past tense because he was unique for a time and era we shall never see again. Here, the people mourn the lost era of the South. I mourn that marvelous era of Western heritage that may be remembered only for its gunslingers. But, the sun is warm and believe it or not, I still freckle up with too much sun. Have you supper plans, Mr. Breed?"

Nate was taken aback by her quick change of subject. "I am hardly off the train and must go back to find lodging."

"Nonsense! You have already found it. We would welcome your company at the plantation. I, too, keep Teton Jack on hand for the times when Preacher would pay a quiet visit to Brent and myself."

Nate was crestfallen. "Then you supplied the Teton Jack for today."

"Hardly," she laughed. "That arrived by special carrier from New Orleans. Ordered by Mrs. Giscard d'Chirac to arrive on this day."

Nate gasped anew. "Jean-Luc Truffaut! Only one man in the world could order her about! Then he has to be alive!"

"Why don't we explore that possibility over supper?"

"Invitation accepted, Mrs. Barrett!"

He felt like a cat fish in a muddy spring stream. Was the worm on the water's surface swimming on its own or attached to an angler's hook. He had to rise to the bait, no matter what. Because, whether he learned the truth of Preacher being alive that day or not, it was important to learn about the mysterious, missing years of James David Preacher from Morgana. The Civil War years, which Preacher had kept as close to his chest as an inside straight at the poker table.

CHAPTER 1

Bradburn Hill - October, 1861

THE BREATH OF frost came into the air. The leaves of all but
the evergreens were splashed with great masses of fire bright
colors. The chockcherry bushes were bright with purple
berries and the ground a sea of violent hues as the fallen
leaves flowed over the land in yellow and orange and vibrant
red.

Hunting parties found ample supplies of wild game.
Daniel Colridge Preacher and James David Preacher were
often seen together hunting the vast acres and woodlands of
the Bradburn Hill plantation, but never in the farm
community of Bradburn Hill. Matilda Polk Preacher
demanded it be that way. As tiny, forceful and fiery as she
was, she still smarted when some would still call her youngest
son a murderer. Some, whom she had known all their lives,
she stopped speaking to and refused to sell them her prize
horse stock, and that included the people at Langhorne Oaks.

Dan Preacher took things quieter. He, too, at age fifteen,
had to take on the full chores of manhood. His mentor as a
marksman and tracker had been Davy Crockett. In his heart
he knew that James David had killed Calvin Fuller protecting
Preacher property. He also knew his son had started a county-
wide war with the sheriff among the dead. Every death, in
that little war, had been put at his son's feet. Still, he was
having a hard time getting to know his son again.

In April, when they had sent him away to keep him from a
lynch mob, he had been but fifteen. To protect him they had
given him the birthing papers of Jeremiah Preacher, Dan and
Matilda's stillborn first child. The papers had made him

twenty years old for the record. The experiences encountered in those six months had made him twenty in mind and fact.

"Dad, I've got to talk something out, so Ma doesn't hear. Michael Langhorne sent a Charles Barrington after me, but his real name was Charley Barr, the fast-draw gunman. Don't ask me how, but I outdrew him and took on his identity. Missouri was a mess, Dad. Morgan Lake got ahold of me and taught me how to protect myself and survive. I've left a trail of dead men behind me that I don't even want to count. But I want you to know that I never killed in cold-blood. The part that really troubles me is being called a Widow Maker."

"I think I know that feeling, son. Back in 1830, when Indian trouble erupted around here, I fretted over the lives I was taking."

"But they were savages."

"No more savage than the men you seem to have been facing. Still men, with squaws and children. If a man takes up arms against another man, it is upon his soul if he is going to leave behind a widow and fatherless children. I'm glad you brought Morgana Lake home with you. I like that girl, and I like the things she has said about you. Do you have an interest in that direction?"

Six months before he would have blushed at such a question. Now he looked his father square in the eye. "We were intimate, Pa, but determined we were better off as brother and sister."

Dan Preacher nodded. He was faced with a very mature young son, and he was proud. But there was still a thorn in his heart. "Can we now discuss Zachary?"

Preacher's handsome face clouded. "Pa, I've always loved and respected Zach. I even used to idolize him and try to be like him in every way. I'm still confused as to what part he played with Michael Langhorne in the illegal slaves sales and my near death in New Orleans. It's like the time you took the two of us to the Alamo." He laughed.

Dan was happy to hear his natural laugh again, too.

"I told the people in Missouri that was my first time away from home. I hadn't forgotten about that trip to the Alamo for the twentieth anniversary of the battle. Back then, I thought the Alamo was a part of Tennessee just because Davy

Crockett was born fifteen miles from here.''

Then he grew serious again. ''There has been an animosity between Zach and me since that trip. If that is still gnawing on Zach, I'll hold my peace.''

''And what of Michael Langhorne?''

Preacher grinned broadly. ''Pa, I was about ten when the cotton tonnage was coming up short of your calculations. You didn't say a word, but your eyes made one man feel guilty enough to confess to the theft. You fired Patrick Donner over that.''

Dan sighed. ''Best foreman I ever had.''

''And you were soft hearted enough to let him keep the profits from the stolen cotton to buy land and set up his own farm. You had all the evidence against him.''

Dan Preacher bristled. ''And, from what I understand, you have the same against Michael Langhorne!''

Preacher rose and stretched. ''I am my father's son. I have the evidence, he has the guilt.''

Dan Preacher grinned. ''So, my old rule, smoke them out with silence.'' He became serious.

''What of Rosamond? Aren't you hurting an innocent party, as well?''

Bitterness turned Preacher's mouth downward. ''Did he think of what it might do to Mother and Abigail when he had Fuller try to steal our slaves? Did he think of his wife and daughter when they nursed me back to health and he ordered a man to ride after me and kill me? Besides, Rosamond is not the only girl in my life.'' He suddenly turned fifteen again, in the company of his father. ''Oh, no sir, I have never been intimate with Rosamond.''

Dan Preacher wanted to laugh, but dared not. He put a stern look on his face. ''Jeremy, five years elapsed between the time I met your mother and we were married. I was hardly celibate for all those years. Still, I was cautious. I greatly question your caution with one Betsy Fuller, as your brother denies all.''

James David Preacher had never had a chance to deny or explain. It now poured out in one long sentence. Coming upon the Fuller men stealing Bradburn Hill slaves . . .

tracking them to the foreman's house . . . granting sexual favors to Betsy Fuller for information because she thought she was bedding with his brother Zachary . . . and finally the gun duel with Calvin to win the freedom of their slaves and the Barrett's studman Luke.

"Pa, I don't think that is my kid she is carrying, but if it is, tell me what to do that is proper."

Dan Preacher stood silent for a moment. One son denied, which made him greatly suspect. Another son confessed and asked for the proper thing for him to do. Tears came to his eyes, but he turned so Jeremy would not see them.

"You will do nothing, Jeremy. It is my understanding that Collin Young thinks the child is also his and has quietly let Henry Fuller know he will marry her."

"Does Betsy know?"

"I assume she does. She has not hounded me with her foolish demands since I made my bargain."

"What bargain?"

"She was to stop her charges that you or Zach fathered her child, in exchange for letting Henry Fuller live out the season in the foreman's house and drop charges against you as the killer of Calvin."

"Was that before or after you learned I was in New Orleans?"

"New Orleans? That came no more than a month after you left. Zachary had Michael Langhorne wire a Mr. McPhee and a Mr. Trotter in Sikeston that you were free to come home. You wired back that you were in training with the Missouri militia and would be home at the end of summer."

Preacher's heart went cold. His brother Zachary again. It was too soon to let his father know what evidence he had on his brother. But the beautiful moments just spent with his father had all turned sour.

Day after day they continued to hunt, but the conversation level was as silent as the woods.

The autumn air was filled with the pungent aroma of the smoke house preparing hams and bacon sides for the winter. Venison and bear meat was cut thin for jerky smoking. Late summer corn had been gathered, dried and ground into

meal. The orchards had been picked clean and the fruits
canned and stored in the fruit cellars. Cotton had been
picked, combed, baled and shipped for passage to English
mills. For the first time in the nation's young history, no
cotton went to New England mills. They stood idle, their
workers stunned and not understanding this stupid war.

"Hateful! You are all being just hateful!" Abigail pouted.
"The Langhorne Oaks fall barbeque is the best social thing
until Christmas. Rosamond rode over special with a personal
invitation. She was greatly put out that a certain young man
was off hunting with Papa. Mama, please? Oh, please?"

"It is up to your father," Matilda said coolly.

"Well, Mattie," Dan said slowly, "Jeremy and I have been
giving this a lot of consideration, while we were hunting.
Right, son?"

Preacher remained poker faced and watched a scowl grow
on Zachary's face.

Dan spread his big red hands out on the table. "If we
don't show up, we are subject to gossip from those who are
pro-Union. If we do show up, we are subject to gossip from
those who are pro-South."

"It's still two weeks away," Matilda said softly, so softly
that every family member turned to eye her. They all knew
that she longed for her deep friendship with Elsie Langhorne.
"Doesn't seem proper having such a social to-do, but I'll
invite Elsie over for tea and discuss it. Two weeks is a long
time away, nowadays."

Two weeks was not long enough for some people.

"How do you know he will even accept the Langhorne
invitation, Sheriff? I say we ride onto Preacher land and call
him out to avenge the killing of Clyde Donner!"

Sheriff Collin Young spat, the tobacco juice pinging on the
edge of the spitoon. "All you would be doing, Mack, is give
Dan Preacher an open invitation to shoot us for trespassing."

"How could he do that when you are the sheriff and I'm
your deputy?"

"Mack, you're an ass!" He looked out the fly-specked
window of the jail house. "Judge Harland George slapped us

good when we rode onto Preacher land in April and thought we had killed the Preacher kid. Said I had no authority to order such a raid as an Acting Sheriff. I am still just *acting* until the election in November.''

"But the judge signed the papers for Clyde Donner to go to New Orleans and arrest the Preacher kid.''

Collin Young turned and eyed Michael "Mack" McDuffy in the same manner that Sheriff McColum used to eye him. Deputies were to take orders and keep their mouths shut. "Mack, don't you ever say that in public. Judge George signed nothing. I forged those papers. Michael Langhorne had me make it look like Carter House was the deputy I sent to New Orleans. he knew that James David would trust Patrick House's son.''

"That was clever,'' Mack grinned, "because you knew Carter had left for the war the day before.'' He frowned. "He and Clyde Donner rode off to war together. How did you get ahold of Clyde to go to New Orleans for you?''

Young didn't answer. Clyde had ridden away with Carter House and led him right into an ambush set up by Collin Young and Michael Langhorne. Langhorne wanted Carter silenced because he was one of the men who murdered Barclay Barrett. Young wanted Carter dead because he found out he was one of the men who had been secretly sleeping with Betsy Fuller. Clyde Donner he could trust to kill Preacher in New Orleans and then disappear into the army.

But the report he had received from the New Orleans' authorities had made him sick and more hateful towards James David Preacher. The shootout had been in the *Maison Blanc*, a New Orleans' whorehouse. Donner had been rash, even though backed up by New Orleans' constables. To a man they said that young Preacher had acted in self defense and then vanished. They buried the dead man under the name of Carter House.

As far as the county people knew, Carter House and Clyde Donner were off at war.

The truth that it was Donner in New Orleans rested with Mack, Sheriff Young, Langhorne, Zachary Preacher, and James David—because he was there.

Mack was still puzzled. "What's going to happen when

the Donner and House families don't hear from Carter or Clyde?''

Collin Young eyed his deputy for a long moment. Mack was not the brightest man in the world, although he followed his orders well. But once in awhile, like right now, he came up with a right interesting question.

''Good point, Mack. Langhorne wants us to steer clear of the Preacher kid because he fears that he may have brought back too much evidence from Missouri to tie him and us into the illegal slave operation.''

''Hell, Zach Preacher was up to his neck, too!''

''Right you are,'' Collin grinned, ''and I'm getting a little sick of taking orders from the high and mighty Mr. Langhorne. Time we started looking at things our way. How long have Dan Preacher and Patrick House been feuding over that hickory wood ridge between their lands?''

The heavy set man shrugged. ''Ever since Matilda Preacher inherited Bradburn Hill from her pappy. Over twenty years. But how does that help us?''

Young grinned. ''No one knows the truth, so I can make up my own truth. I think it's time to let Patrick House know I sent his son to New Orleans to arrest James David Preacher. Hell, that was only late August. A month for an official report to reach me ain't unusual. And where was I week before last?''

''In Charleston trying to get the army to give you military authority here.''

''Right, as far as you know. Wrong for everyone else. I was in New Orleans straightening out this confusing report. They had to exhume the body and I was shocked to learn that it was Clyde Donner. Since my return I have been quietly investigating. We learned James David was in New Orleans from his brother Zach. Zach knew that I was sending Carter House. Only one man could have substituted Clyde Donner for Carter House.''

Mack whistled, ''His great drinking buddy, Zachary Preacher.''

''And Pat House won't be saying a word to Kevin Donner, because he hates him worse than Dan Preacher. We'll give it a few days to let the words fly between the old men and then we will find Carter's grave.''

"How is that going to help?"

"Langhorne and I made sure we buried him on Preacher land.''

Mack scratched his beard, pondering. ''Sounds good, except for Zach. He knows too damn much about too damn many things. What if he starts opening his drunken mouth?''

Young grinned broadly. ''Exactly, Mack. I hope that he does. Zach Preacher is no longer any good to us. If he makes trouble, we'll take him out.''

"You or me?''

"Either one,'' he said in a dull voice. ''We need this feud. The House family are as hard-nosed pro-Union as Zach Preacher is a rabble-rousing Reb. No matter what happens, the report I'll send to Charleston and Richmond will force them to put us under military authority. I'll then show these holier-than-thou people that they can't call me a cracker anymore.''

Daniel Preacher listened to his wife's carping. He was blunt in his response. ''Jeremy says it is subterfuge to get him to do gun battle. He does not think Zachary is capable of killing. It may hurt your sensitive ears, Matilda, but I always thought Zach more capable of killing that James David. I resent Collin Young playing tattle-tale and not making open accusations. And, because Michael Langhorne's name is again connected, you may tell Elsie we shall not set foot on their property.''

He rose and took the case of dueling pistols from their hiding place. ''I have tried reaching Patrick House with words of reason, he demands this. I shall still try reason. I have asked James David to be my second. Patrick has asked, of all people, Michael Langhorne. If neither your son nor I return, you will know it was a dirty trap, which I fully suspect. If I am correct, have Juice Harp drive you and Abigail to your family. Leave our burial to Zachary. It might make him think what he has brought about.''

Matilda Preacher sat stunned. It was a cold, foggy October

morning. The night before there had been blood on the moon. She hated the dueling brace of pistols. They had brought death before. They would bring death again.

CHAPTER 2

THE FOG WAS so thick in the pasture that the men could hardly see each other ten feet apart. They had fought a word battle for over an hour. Preacher thought Michael Langhorne presented the House case with reasonable logic, although walking a fine line between truth and fiction to save his own neck. Daniel was more than pleased with his son as counsel. Without a doubt, they were all convinced that it had been Clyde Donner who had perished in New Orleans. But Patrick House was Welsh to the last drop of his blood. He seemed to care little about his dead son, only satisfaction over an acre of wooded land he claimed as his and stolen by Daniel Preacher. Neither Langhorne nor James David could bring him back to reason on the feud at hand. He arrogantly marched off his ten paces and demanded Daniel do the same.

Daniel Preacher was just into his eighth step when House screamed.

"You're a dead Irishman, Preacher!"

There was a shot. Preacher spun and drew. Patrick House stood stunned, the pistol still at the side of his leg. Daniel Preacher groaned and began to fall.

"What the hell!" Langhorne screamed.

There was another shot. It came from the stand of hickory trees which the fog made look like a silent watching audience.

Patrick House screamed, caught at his chest and fell.

Flashes of fire from a half dozen guns came from the woods. Preacher fired back, with both of his guns, but knew he was hitting nothing.

There was a whine of a rifle. Langhorne cried out and clutched at his leg. There was another barrage of pistol shots. They made House's already dead body jump all over the pasture.

Preacher knew exactly what he had to do, how fast he had to do it. He stood up, let out a death rattling yell and collapsed.

"Mr. Langhorne," he whispered, "don't move or make a sound. They don't want any witnesses to this ambush and think they have us all wounded or dead. They'll sneak out to check on us in a moment."

"Who are they?"

Preacher didn't answer. He didn't want to answer. Zach had not been home the night before, although he knew of the pending duel. Who gained more by the death of the four of them than Zach?

He had fallen in a tall patch of hay that had not been reaped. It gave him cover to reload his pistols. They were the ones he had taken off Charles Barrington after out-drawing him. The finely crafted German weapons had become his closest friends in the last six months. He waited.

Mack McDuffy pulled his 280 pounds up into the saddle and motioned his three brothers to do the same. Sheriff Young had reasoned that Dan Preacher and Pat House would wound or kill each other. All Mack would have to do was finish them off and take care of Langhorne and young Preacher. Mack was unsure of himself, so he brought his brothers as a back-up. Now he rode forward with confidence. He had not really needed his brothers.

McDuffy stopped by the riddled body of House. His brothers were some forty feet behind him. Preacher thought one shot might disperse them. He aimed low. The bullet struck Mack on the left knee, shattered kneecap, joint tendons, muscle and bone. Amazingly, he stayed in his saddle, although screaming like a banshee.

It did not disperse his brothers, but made them come riding to his aid. Langhorne saw Preacher's intent. He, too, aimed only for legs or pistol held arms. He, more than Preacher, wanted them to ride away alive. He had recognized

McDuffy and smelled Collin Young behind this murderous attempt. He would see them all hang.

Once each brother had tasted of a bullet, they left silently. Just as silently, Preacher helped Langhorne to his horse and then carried his father home in his arms. Daniel Preacher was unconscious and James David wept at the sight of the devastating wound. Once his father was in the hands of his mother, he sent Amos to gather in the body of Patrick House, and Juice Harp was sent to fetch Judge Harland George.

Sheriff Collin Young pulled order out of chaos quickly. He nicely tied Judge George's hands. Dueling was illegal in Tennessee and he had sent a deputy and *three men* out to stop the bloodbath. They found even the seconds firing upon each other, and then they were fired upon and wounded. Because he considered it a Civil War feud, he had ordered martial law and called in the army.

The county and townspeople snickered over his charges and then a wave of indignation and horror swept over all of Eastern Tennessee. Collin Young's report had been brutal, savage and greatly distorted. The Confederate Army marched in and treated the region like conquered enemy territory. Farms were looted for food. People were turned out of their homes to house officers. Fields were turned into army tent camps and orchards chopped down for fire wood. Slaves were confiscated to become army slaves. Women were raped because they were considered enemy women.

A curtain of silence fell over Bradburn Hill plantation and Langhorne Oaks. Each had men recuperating from wounds. But the indignation penetrated even the sick chamber of Daniel Preacher, lying almost helpless from a ghastly wound to the shoulder which Sheriff Young claimed came from the pistol of Patrick House.

"Heathen!" Daniel roared. "Jeff Davis is a heathen to send Confederate troops here and treat us as though we were the enemy! No, Matilda! His officers cannot have any of your horses until they pay in gold!"

"Their printed money is good, Pa," Zachary said in his usual monotone. "This Troop Commander is quite fair.

Better than the people are getting in Johnson City. Pa, rather than go join a military outfit in Georgia, I might be of more use right here. Collin Young is becoming quite a little dictator. A home boy, like me, with this new Commander, might keep Collin in line.''

James David Preacher idled against the fireplace in his father's bedroom, watching his mother change the dressing on the wound. Out of respect for his mother, neither he, nor his father, had voiced what part Zachary might have played in their duel ambush. Only to Morgana Lake, their houseguest, had Preacher poured out his suspicions and doubts about Zach. But, he could not remain fully silent.

"Seems to me," he said slowly, "you'd make a fine specimen for that troop, Zach. Good broad shoulders, fine physique, good legs and . . ." he looked up at the ceiling . . . "you seem to know a lot of secrets that could bottle and cork ole Collin Young.''

"You may believe me or not," Zach said apathetically, "but the man lies as much about me as he does about you, James David. I have done nothing to bring you harm, brother," he smoothly lied. "I am not the one who brought shame on the family by becoming a gunslinger.''

Preacher almost laughed. Zach was still treating him like a fifteen year old. He could crush his brother in his parents' eyes, but the time was not right. This should have been the autumn of his youth. Zach, through Michael Langhorne, had changed his life, perhaps forever. They had put guns in his hands. They had caused him to kill or be killed. They had made him the Widow Maker. He could never be fifteen again, or even Jeremy's twenty. He was older, much older. You don't kill a man and stay young.

"Problem is the present," he said drily, "not past. Patrick House is dead and they say Pa did it. I know that is bullshit. This Captain Kelley only has Collin Young's version, through Mack McDuffy—''

"And I can straighten that all out, Pa, if you would—''

"Will you shut up, Zach! I'll straighten it out, because I was there! I'll answer because I don't fear the truth and have no reason to lie!''

Zach raised his face. It was filled with astonishment. He no longer knew his brother. The change in James David was obvious.

"Pa, it isn't right." Zach protested. "He is only a kid and I am the heir and should be the spokesman before Captain Kelley!"

"He was man enough to save my life!"

"Goddamit! Will you start facing reality. He can't handle the past. That's what Collin Young got out of Patrick House. Not the death of his son! Not a stupid quarrel over that hickory woodland. Merrit House! That's what Young gave Kelley and he is licking his chops over that little county scandal!"

Daniel turned so ashen Preacher feared his father was dying. His mother turned a look on his brother that was murderous. Then she turned on him and looked like hammered iron.

"If they know, then you must know."

"Mother," Zachary barked. "Let the men of the family decide this matter!"

"It was my matter," she said coldly, "and don't you ever speak to me in that tone again. I resent it. I also resent that James David has lost his bubble of youth. In its place is a grown man, with a soft voice, a hard eye and no hint of fear. That's why he must know. Although, I question how you knew, Zachary. I will speak to you alone on that subject in a moment. But, James David, Merrit House, was Patrick House's older brother. He was a fine horse breeder and taught me all I knew. He was a fine, handsome man and took my Irish zest for life to mean something more. One day in the stables he raped me and demanded I leave your father. I could not, and he demanded a duel. Your father won. I put those pistols away, for what I thought was forever. You, of course, forced Mama Dee to get them out when you went after Calvin Fuller. When Amos brought them back from the pasture, neither had been fired. I took them out to the blacksmith shop and hid them. I hoped they would never kill again. I wish I could do the same with your weapons. But, for the moment, you are the son I wish to talk to this Confederate Captain. Zachary, I will see you in my bedroom, at once!"

CHAPTER 3

FOR MORE THAN a week after his lengthy conversation with Jeremy James David Preacher, Captain Andrew Kelley withdrew from contact with Sheriff Collin Young and began his own private investigation. He soon began to feel that the lawman has used him, and his troops, for personal revenge motives and not military.

Command of a troop, so far from home, was a startling revelation for Andrew Kelley. He had been Commander of the Atlanta Home Guard over men he knew. Here in Tennessee he was commanding strangers with little or no military training and a resentment toward the plantation rich equal only to their hatred of the blacks.

As an Atlanta businessman, he had always considered the enslavement of black people as harsh, cruel and potentially dangerous. The troublesome plantations—according to Young's report—he found peaceful, quiet, productive and the slaves well cared for in body and mind. On the plantations that were to be left alone, especially Langhorne Oaks, he saw cruel treatment and the killing of the slaves' will and pride. He and his men became the enemy of all.

"Captain," Young sneered. "It is my county and if you can't control your men, I can!"

"I strongly question it was my men in that tavern brawl. They are Georgia farmers and woodsmen and look little different to me than some of the men around here."

"I know every man for a hundred miles around. Best you start learning your men."

His home guard had no uniforms and he was struggling to

learn their names and faces. In Johnson City he hit upon a plan. At Hanson's Mercantile he bought a bolt of red cloth and cut it into kerchief triangles. Now he could tell his men from the locals. The cotton bolt had been cheaply dyed. The kerchiefs clung wetly to the neck skin and the dye ran. It did not wash out of the skin easily and stained necks soon replaced the kerchiefs.

"What are the rednecks up to, today?"

"Tried to take control of the Barrett place."

"Why?"

"Sheriff Young told them it was illegal for Luke Barrett to run the place because he's still a niggah."

"What happened?"

"That big buck chased them off with his Sharpes rifle!"

"That's the white Barrett blood in him coming out."

It was good cracker barrel gossip for Lungston's General Store.

"About the time someone put that snooty Captain Kelley in his place."

"He weren't there. Off with part of the troop in Walkertown. Young said he was in charge of them and sent them out there with Henry Fuller."

This brought snickers.

"What's Collin want to do, put his future father-in-law in charge of that plantation?"

"You telling me that Collin is goin' ta marry that Betsy Fuller?"

"Ain't you seen her lately? She's got one in the oven that must be six ta seven months along."

"Ain't Collin's kid, as I hear tell. My woman tells me she hounded ole Dan Preacher, claiming it was either Zach or James David."

"Preacher boys? Naugh. Oh, I could believe such of that drunken Zachary, but the young'un was sent to Missouri because he killed Calvin Fuller and got Jamie Fuller killed on that raid of the Preacher place."

"Jeb is right. You don't go around sleeping with a man who put both your brothers in their graves."

Such gossip was also common in Hartley's Tavern, but of a coarser nature because it could not be overheard by the women shoppers. Except for those afternoons when Zachary Preacher was a customer, which was becoming almost daily.

That afternoon the low buzz of gossip centered around Zach's drinking partner. Collin Young had spread the word very effectively that it was Clyde Donner who had been killed in New Orleans and not Carter House. But there was Zach, getting drunker by the moment, pouring drinks into Fitzgerald Donner.

Jerry Donner, on first hearing of his brother's fate, had been incredulous. Then, with anguished eyes, he sought out Clyde's old drinking buddy, Zachary Preacher.

"My family thought Clyde was off to the war. Collin lied to us, Zach, and says you knew."

"Knew," Zach scoffed. "He's also saying I'm the only one who could have killed Carter House. Shit, Jerry, I ain't ever killed anyone in my life."

"But what do you know?"

Zach smiled drunkenly. Ever since he had heard Jerry wanted to meet with him, he had been carefully plotting. He had stalled until this day, for a very important reason.

"I know I am tired of being the Preacher family ass and taking all the blame. Hell, if Clyde were alive, he could tell you that it was Collin who was screwin' around with Betsy. You know I put my pecker into better meat than that. I was at Longhorne Oaks when my little brother brought about that niggah uprising and Collin says I was to blame because I was trying to sell some of my father's slaves. Hell, Jerry, your old man owns near a hundred slaves. Clyde and I did everything together. Could he have figured out a way to steal Donner slaves and sell them behind your old man's back?"

Jerry Donner shook his head and tried to focus his eyes. "Couldn't be done. Not on my old man."

Zachary threw another shot of corn liquor down his throat. "Nor on my old man, but that's what I am accused of by my little brother and Collin Young. Collin I can understand. He don't want no shotgun wedding over Betsy and will stick me with any dirt he can think up. But, my baby brother? Well, I found out something recently that makes me think he's not a true Preacher."

Donner blinked. "What were that?"

Zachary drew him close, but made sure the bartender could hear his full answer. "The Preacher-House feud! This wasn't the first time a Preacher and a House have dueled, Jerry. My father first dueled Merritt House because he raped my mother and then along comes little James David. Doesn't my hot tempered little brother remind you a hell of a lot of that worthless House clan? You know how your family felt when Carter House wanted to marry your sister Elvira. Your old man wanted no Donner and House bloods mixing."

"Damn right!" Jerry fumed. "Pa cussed for a week because Clyde was seen riding off to war with that worthless Carter House. If'n you killed him, Zach, you're my man. But, why would your brother shoot down Clyde in cold blood?"

Zach scowled. "Jerry, I no longer claim him as a brother. Humph! Look at this last duel. My father almost killed, and House killed, but neither dueling pistol fired. Langhorne wounded? My brother claims it was McDuffy on Collin's orders. Bull crap! Michael Langhorne saw no one else there but my brother. Now, he's too frightened to say anything against James David. He thinks he was to be left for dead, too, but McDuffy arrived too soon to see what all the shooting was about."

Donner's eyes were popping. "But, why would he try to kill Langhorne?"

Zach grinned wickedly. "To keep Langhorne quiet on the illegal slave trade and the murder of Carter House."

Donner burped. "That still don't account for him wounding your dad."

Zach thought a long moment, playing out his game. "Good way of keeping the secret of his birth a secret. Clyde knew that secret, too."

"How in the hell did he know?"

Zach shrugged. "I don't rightly know, but how in the hell do you think I found out about it?"

"Goddam, I'm beginning to hate your brother!"

Zachary Preacher poured them each another shot of corn liquor. Like the liquor, he was very pleased with the bold faced lies he continued to pour on these troubled waters. He knew that Jerry Donner was an excellent shot, drunk or sober.

Jerry Donner was itching to get into the war, but with four boys already fighting for the south, and Clyde now dead, Anna Donner refused to let her hothead youngster leave home. Zach also knew that his own mother disallowed his brother to wear any of the arms he had brought back from Missouri. He checked his pocket watch and smiled.

Matilda Preacher had ordered Zach to bring James David to town in the surrey for a meeting with Captain Kelley. Hartley's Tavern had been the location suggested for their meeting. A moment before, through the open tavern doors, he had seen Judge Harland George return to his law office. He took that as a sign that the meeting was over. Then into his view he saw the Fuller farm wagon pull up and Betsy Fuller climb down from the high seat. Henry Fuller rolled the wagon on, looking neither left nor right. The loss of two sons, and an unwed pregnant daughter had left him pinch-mouthed and hateful to the world.

Betsy Fuller stopped dead still. Her face screwed up into a gathering storm cloud. Zach chuckled over his profound luck, for crossing the street toward the tavern were James David and Captain Kelley. He longed to hear what would transpire, but had to keep Jerry Donner's attention away from that trio until James David entered the tavern.

"Captain Kelley," Betsy hissed, "I hope this means you finally have this killer under arrest!"

"I have no grounds to arrest him, Miss Fuller."

The storm exploded. "Nothing? Another Preacher buy-off? So, he is to remain free to kill and kill again. You men make me sick! You are so blind!" She spat.

It did not reach Preacher's face, but landed on the toe of his boot. He ignored it and stared hard into her eyes.

His stare did not silence Betsy. "Murder is not his only crime, Captain," she continued to scoff. "Look at me! I consider it a crime that he can crawl between my legs and then his father refuses to believe that I carry his grandchild."

"If that fact were true, Miss Fuller," Kelley said sternly, "I question why Sheriff Collin Young is scheduling a wedding date and calling the child his own."

Betsy Fuller's face turned crimson. "Do not impose yourself on a local matter, sir!"

Normally, Andy Kelley was a gentleman, with strict family upbringing. As a twenty-five year old bachelor, he found the subject of the conversation troubling and embarrassing on a public street.

"You raised the subject," he said, as though each word were a thrown dart. "I do not believe in adultery or infidelity, but in my official capacity here I have learned a few of the sordid details. As you do not seem prone to be lady-like, and keep private matters from being discussed on the main street, let me be candid. I have a full accounting of your one meeting with James David Preacher, when in actual fact you mistook him for his brother, whom you seemed to have met several times in a less than sober condition. I would hardly call Sheriff Young a gentleman when he has let me know that he was meeting secretly with you almost nightly during that period of time."

"It was not nightly," she snapped. "Only on the night's Sheriff McCullum wanted Collin out of the way for—" She stopped short.

Her Fuller temper had nearly gotten her into trouble again. If James David had not killed Sheriff McCullum during the raid of the Preacher place, things would be a lot different. He had been a terror of a lawman. He would have been able to prove it was a Preacher seed in her. But neither Collin nor this wimpy Captain would help her. Oddly, Collin wanted her as a bride, although she did not want him as a groom. Now she felt a door closing and the Preacher money slipping through her fingers. She would accept her fate, but never cease to plot Preacher's revenge.

She stalked away to the general store.

"Oh, by the way," Kelley said, as though trying to change the subject. "Thank your mother for the dinner invitation she sent by Miss Abigail. I most gratefully accept. Best you now get Zachary to take you back home. Young and his deputies are due back soon."

Reluctantly, he entered the tavern to find Zach. Taverns now reminded him too much of shootouts. To him they all now smelled of tobacco, stale beer, burnt powder and warm blood. He also felt naked without leather and metal riding heavy on his hips. It took a second for his eyes to adjust to the internal gloom and spot his brother leaning over the bar.

"Zach, time to go," he said softly.

"No!" The bark was drunken and challenging. "For your time has run out, Preacher, boy!"

Preacher kept momentarily silent and calm. He was defenseless and in the worst position possible. The challenger stood in shadowy gloom, while he was a full target silhouetted against the sunbright doorway. He squinted to search out the man and words to use against him. Then he recognized the bulky, handsome figure of Jerry Donner standing next to his brother at the bar.

"I've got no quarrel with you, Jerry."

"But I have with you, buster!" Jerry wove away from the bar and had to reach out for it again to steady himself. "I hear tell you killed my brother in New Orleans!"

Preacher sighed. He had already learned you could not reason with a mind clouded with liquor. He did not have to suspect who had clouded this mind with liquor. His brother's face was a mask of sweat beads and anticipation.

"Well, Jerry," he drawled, taking his time to check the weapons Jerry carried in his twin holsters and who else in the tavern bore weapons and could be considered friendly, enemy or neutral.

"Well, what? You bastard child!"

Zach cringed and reached for his drink with a shaking hand. Jerry had said too much, too soon.

Preacher's ears were as sharp as his eyes. He heard and saw two reactions. Erik Hartley, behind the bar, continued to polish glasses as though he had heard nothing. Every other man in the tavern hunkered their heads down over their drinks, except for one. Jerry Donner stood grinning, licking his lips in part fear and part delight. Preacher had seen that before, too many times. Gun fighting was like lust. Preacher could almost taste Donner's desire to kill him, and all he could tell him was truth.

"It was Clyde in New Orleans, Jerry, when I thought it was going to be Carter House. He wasn't there to arrest me, but to bring me back home in a pinewood box to avenge the deaths of Calvin and Jamie because of Hanna Fuller."

Donner blanched. "Shut up! That's family secret stuff!"

"When it nearly takes my life I don't give a shit who knows that Hannah Fuller is your sister and she married Henry Fuller before your family moved here. Nor was it a shootout. Clyde came at me from behind with a Bowie knife and I have a shoulder scar to prove my point. He played as dirty as you are playing now. I have no weapon, and a roomful of witnesses will testify to that fact."

"You bastard!" Donner slurred. "I want everyone to know he's a lying bastard! Do you think my Pa would let one of his daughters marry a worthless scum like Henry Fuller. That's reason enough for me to kill you!"

"Hardly!" Preacher barked, seeing a couple of the men were starting to doubt him. "I still stand unarmed to your challenge. Time for you to back down, go home and sober up."

There were murmurs of agreement when Zachary screamed out and spun. "No! A Preacher does not walk away from a duel challenger!" From under his coat he produced a four-shot vest pocket pistol and threw it at his brother.

Preacher caught the weapon in mid-flight and froze. Donner could draw and fire at any second, and all could claim Preacher had a weapon in his hand. He had been set-up. He was a dead patsy and he felt as sick inside as the day Charles Barrington had taught him to fast draw and then challenged him. He was looking sure death square in the face.

The freeze position, with the caught weapon in his up raised right hand was only for a second, then he expertly tossed the light weight gun over to his left hand. It stalled Donner's draw and caught the attention of his eyes. Thereafter Preacher did not take his eyes off the man's hands. His left hand, as surely as his right hand, had minds of their own. They did not need his eyes to aim and fire. His eyes had a more important task to perform. The moment Preacher's eyes saw Donner's hands close down over the pistol hilts, he fired, spun to his right as he fanned the hammer of the piece, and fired again. Jerry Donner's hands never got the pistols out of the hilts of the sheath leather.

There was a sudden silence in the room, a frozen tableau as though captured on canvas by oil paint. They all waited for

Jerry Donner to fall with a death rattle, but he remained standing with a stupidly foolish look upon his face.

He knew he was alive, but his hands felt numb and strange on the gun butts. He lifted them and was amazed to see that the palm of each had been shattered by a bullet. Only when the blood began to flow did his throat erupt with a weeping wail.

The gunshots and wail had brought Captain Andrew Kelley back on the run with pistol drawn. He masked his amazement at the scene and came up slowly to Preacher and put out his hand. Preacher gave him the pistol without hesitation.

"Is this yours, son?"

"It certainly is not!" Zachary declared quickly, disgusted with Donner for not killing Preacher, and needing to cover his tracks quickly. "It is mine, and now that my brother is finished with it, I shall have it back, if you please!"

A smile flickered across the Captain's stern, fine face. "I don't please, for the moment." He broke open the weapon and removed the two empty shells. There were no cartridges in the other two chambers. Kelley frowned.

"What in the hell is going on here?" Collin Young demanded, storming into the tavern, followed by a hobbling Mack McDuffy. "Kelley, whose gun is that? Donner, what in the hell happened to your hands?"

"That bastard shot them!" he wailed, pointing at Preacher.

Young grinned gleefully and McDuffy looked vindictive. "I've been waiting for you to make a slip like this, James David Preacher. March your ass out of here and down to my office."

"Hold it!" Kelley snapped. "I was the first law officer on the scene and no one leaves till I'm finished with my investigation."

Collin's jaw dropped. He had just seen Betsy in the mercantile store and learned that the Captain was siding with the Preacher family and accepting invitations to dine at the plantation. He was tired of being made to look foolish by this army wimp.

"No!" he stormed. "It is not an army matter. McDuffy,

take this bastard to the jail, while I take Donner to the doctor. I heard and seen all I need for my investigation."

"Have you?"

A voice boomed down from the balcony, ringing the second floor of the tavern. A snow-white haired gentleman, in a snow-white suit sat and glared down at them. The barkeep tried to wave his eighty-year old father off, but Baron Hartley would have his say. Daily, he sat at his balcony table and nursed a double shot of bourbon from opening to closing. Since his boys had become old enough to tend the bar, he had been pushed farther and farther out of dealing with the customers.

Customers. The first time the tavern had started making money again was with the arrival of the Georgia Home Guard. He might lose some money in losing a Zach Preacher or Jerry Donner, but he would rather side with the handsome, young army officer.

"Damndest thing I've ever seen," he chirped. "In a duel you go for the heart, not the hands. The boy was challenged and weaponless, till his brother threw him that little toy. Damn smart gun work. That boy is welcome any time, but I don't want to see your faces again, Zach Preacher and Jerry Donner. Which reminds me. What in the hell are you doing in here, Collin Young? I banished you ten years ago and don't recall lifting that ban. Son, set up drinks for the house. Most fun I've had in a coon's age."

As though he had been pistolwhipped by the old man, Collin Young slunk out the door and McDuffy pulled Donner along.

"You know this will get back to Pa." James David said as he and Zach neared Bradburn Hill Plantation.

"I don't see how," Zach said piously, "unless you snitch."

Preacher hesitated, his knuckles itching to taste jaw bone. He glanced at Zach's tousled hair and eyes red with drink. In spite of himself, he felt pity. "Best we keep in mind Pa sips bourbon a couple of times a week with Baron Hartley. Best we go along with the old man's story."

"Best?" Zach sneered, feeling his power returning. "It was truthful and accurate. You were challenged, weaponless and I threw you a pistol to defend yourself.''

"I don't want him ever knowing how you set me up for it,'' Preacher said grimly.

"Don't be absurd,'' Zach said calmly.

"I'm not!'' Preacher's voice was as cold and unemotional as though coming from the pit of a grave. "I just find your drinking partner quite strange, with so much knowledge and hatred. I'm tucking it away, brother, just as I have tucked away all the other facts I have against you.''

"I have done nothing against you!'' Zach protested.

Preacher grinned. It was bone chilling. "To protect the family, I have kept my silence.'' He raised a hand to wave at someone on the plantation porch, but his face or voice never unfroze. "Someday we are going to lock horns so tight they will have to bury us in a common grave.''

Zach sat up straight in the surrey and focused his attention on the young woman waving to them from the porch.

"Of course,'' he whispered to himself, "there is the answer to everything—Morgana Lake.''

Zach had paid little attention to the talk of her pending arrival. She and her father, Morgan Lake, had been more than helpful to James David during his stay in Missouri, and Brent Barrett gave glowing reports of her and her heroic father. When it was learned that James David was coming home, and that Morgan Lake was going to join the forces of Nathan Bedford Forrest, Matilda Preacher invited Morgana Lake to come home with James David for a visit.

The petite firebrand became an instant family hit. Another daughter for Dan and Matilda, a sister for Abigail, and although they sat and talked nightly, it was obvious that Jeremy and Morgana were little more than brother and sister.

But Zachary had never seen her in the family way. His love for her bloomed on first meeting, but they still remained strangers. Every girl he had ever desired he had in a hay loft by the third hello. He still had trouble even saying hello to Morgana.

But that, he now saw, had to cease. Whatever James David knew, he was sure Morgana knew. He could not just blatantly ask her. But with courtship and marriage, what wife could refuse such knowledge to her husband. And by then, he might not need such knowledge, for she was already dearly loved by his mother and father.

"I've been an ass!" he said aloud.

"I'll drink to that!" Preacher said sourly.

Zachary grinned. His comment had nothing to do with his brother, and yet everything to do with his brother. His mind was now set on winning Morgana Lake. And that, in its own way, would also defeat his brother.

CHAPTER 4

THE LOOK ON Morgana's face warned Preacher that Bradburn Hill was already aware of the shootout. He didn't want to face either his mother or father and longed for a quiet corner to sit and chat. She would be the only one to understand that his first thought had been cold enough to go for the heart, but logic had said go for Donner's hands and make an example out of him.

"A messenger just brought this," Morgana said, with a frown.

Preacher was puzzled. The envelope bore the crest of Langhorne Oaks, but his name was not in Rosamond's carefully taught penmanship. He tore open the flap and pulled out the card and his face turned dark at the curtness.

"You are hereby summoned immediately to account for your actions. Michael Langhorne."

"Don't put the surrey away," he growled at his brother. "Mr. Langhorne has something to discuss with me."

Zach paled. "Did he say what?"

Preacher was laconic to hide his wrath. "Nope. Just summoned me like I was one of his slaves. I won't be long."

"You better not be," Morgana warned. "I got a lovely letter from father today and it's filled with news of Brent Barrett and Forrest's Raiders. It almost makes me homesick to be with them."

Preacher grinned to himself. Her face had gone from a frown to cheery happiness. He knew now she had been fretting over the note being from Rosamond. He turned the surrey about and started to ride away. He did not want either to see that he was a little perplexed at being treated like an errant child. He no longer fully feared Michael Langhorne and thought Captain Andrew Kelley had the man pegged: He ruled the roost when Sheriff McCullum was alive, but couldn't fully control Collin Young.

Then Preacher had another thought. When he was being banished from Tennessee, Michael Langhorne had given him a brace of pistols and words of advice: If you sense an enemy, my boy, sit them down and turn them into an ally.

Preacher sensed that the two had become enemies, but saw no way they could be allies.

Zach hesitated, watching Preacher drive away. He feared what knowledge his brother might gain from Langhorne, but felt joy in this opportunity to be alone with Morgana.

"He would make better time if he had saddled his horse," he said, for want of anything else to say.

"I think he wanted the eight miles to get his mind in order. He's been dreading this meeting."

"Are you sure the message wasn't from Rosamond and not her father? He's carried a torch for her since he was eight years old."

"I'm well aware of Miss Rosamond, Zachary, and the other women in Jeremy's life," Morgan laughed.

"Others?" he gasped. "And stop calling him Jeremy."

She laughed again and indicated he should take a seat. "It's hard to call him other than what I knew him as for so long in Missouri. James David makes him sound like someone out of a Bible page. And, please forget my other comment. It was not very ladylike."

"But still uttered in front of me," he scoffed.

"True. Sometimes it's hard being a lady around you, Zach. You are so much like my father. Outwardly hard, cruel and forthright to hide a sensitive interior. I think that is why you so attract me," she added quietly.

"Me?" he laughed cruelly. "We've never passed a single word."

"You started it! You didn't even say hello when we were introduced."

"Because you came here as my brother's girl!"

Morgana bent forward a little, her soft lips smiling. "He and I are like a brother and sister, Zach. I knew that was the way it had to be after the first time we made love. That's the last word I will say about him. If we talk, it will be about us."

Zachary looked at her and smiled with grim mockery. Half a loaf was better than none at all.

It was strange being back at Langhorne Oaks. Preacher had always admired its beauty and knew it was an efficient, reproductive slave farm. There had been a time when he had dreamed of becoming the bridgegroom of Rosamond Langhorne and becoming an heir to this vast wealth. That was before Elsie Langhorne had played surgeon to remove a bullet from his shoulder. That was before he had been a patient in the house, while everyone in the county thought he was dead. That was when he considered Michael Langhorne a friend for making arrangements for him to go to Missouri. It all seemed years ago and not just a few short months.

On the exterior, the sparkling plantation seemed little changed; but internally, it was vastly changed.

Elsie Langhorne, normally warm, bubbling and ready to hear of Bradburn Hill gossip, was cool and remote. Preacher was escorted immediately to Michael Langhorne's study for another surprise. At the duel, he had paid little attention to Michael Langhorne, seeing him as he had always seen him—tall, forceful, with a booming voice that suggested power and demanded respect.

He now sat in a wing-backed chair, his right leg resting on an ottoman and still bandaged from the wound he had received at the duel. He seemed withered, his hair nearly snow white and eyes that darted about as though he was fearful of the world that was changing too rapidly around him.

"Thank you for coming," he nearly whispered. Hardly an opening as curt as his note. "Had the duel ended in a gentlemanly way, I would have asked you a few questions on that day. First, I would like to hear from you, who actually killed Barrington."

Preacher remained standing and eyed the old man as though preparing for a shootout. "I killed your man

Barrington. He tracked me, on your orders, he claimed, and was foolish enough to teach me how to draw with the weapons you had given me. When he called me out, I proved to have been a good student. To survive, I went to Missouri playing the role of Charles Barrington, without knowing that he was actually the infamous gunman Charley Barr. I'm sure your spies kept you informed.''

''Informed?'' he scoffed. ''They had me believing it was Barrington who had turned against me and was ruining a good business venture.''

''How can you call selling stolen slaves a good business venture?''

''I resent that charge!'' His voice broke into a tired quaver. ''For more than a hundred years plantation owners swapped slaves back and forth with papers that you now claim are illegal. My problem was in dealing with horrible little men, with greed, whom I could no longer control.'

Preacher grinned. ''You mean like McPhee, Johnston and Trotter?''

Langhorne looked at him and smiled with his old bravado.

''I was speaking of the little men I have had to deal with here at home. The men you mention are only names to me. I dealt with only one man. Asa Pratt.''

''He's dead.''

''What?'' Langhorne roared. He tried to rise and cringed at the pain in his leg. ''That is impossible! I had a telegram from him two days ago.''

Preacher suddenly feared the man no more. He had the upper hand because of his knowledge. ''The telegram has to be false because Luke Barrett and I were in a shootout with Pratt and the Johnston gang. If you ask me, Jarvis McPhee is the only man who would stoop low enough to use a dead man's name.''

Langhorne laughed until the tears ran down his cheeks.

Outside the door, Rosamond paused with her hand on the knob, hearing the voices coming through. A warning sounded in the hall and she turned and looked questioningly at her mother.

''You didn't tell me James David was coming to call.''

"To see your father," Elsie said sharply. "You will have an opportunity to chat with him. He will be staying for supper and the night."

"The night?"

"The stablemaster has just informed me that his surrey has suddenly developed a broken wheel. Come, let's check on the kitchen."

"I hardly understand your laughter," Preacher growled. "Didn't you stoop low enough to take a dead man's name?"

"That was survival."

"My whole scheme has been survival! Oh, you youthful idiot!" he said with all of his old fury. "This war will be long and weary. The economy of the South is already ruined. I did not intend being among the ruined. Perhaps you have done me more of a service than I realized."

"I beg your pardon?"

"You have spoken the truth, because there was no need to lie. I have sent a fortune in slaves to plantation land in Texas. By next year, I shall have a massive cotton crop to quietly sell to the New England mills. But, I need eyes on that property that I can trust."

Preacher frowned. "I don't think you were listening, Mr. Langhorne. Any slaves that you sent to Missouri were sold."

"Utter nonsense!" he fumed. "My own boy Reggie took the money to Asa Pratt to purchase the Texas land. The reports have been glowing."

"More lies from Jarvis McPhee, would be my answer."

"Then your answer to me has to be a yes."

"Answer? Answer on what?"

"You will return to Missouri as my sole agent to gain back my money, slaves, and land—or kill the men who have so cheated me."

Preacher stared straight ahead. Only a slight quiver up his spine betrayed his rage that Langhorne would even suggest such a thing.

"Now, my boy," Langhorne reasoned with him, "I do have a price for such a service in mind. We both know that I raised an idiot for a son. In no way can I turn over Langhorne Oaks and a new Texas plantation to him. Still, I wish to keep it within the family, say under the care of a son-in-law."

Preacher was stunned. "Does Rosamond know you have such thoughts?"

"Hardly," Michael growled. "It's men business. She will do as she is told. Why don't you go and wash up, stay for supper. Business is better discussed on a full stomach."

Preacher grinned. On the surface he did not trust the man, but supper would mean getting to see Rosamond.

As Preacher stepped out into the hall, he heard the swift clatter of Rosamond's feet as she raced up the stairs. Turning, he looked into Mrs. Langhorne's stricken face.

"You—you've been listening?" Preacher whispered.

"Yes," Elsie sighed. "We were coming from the kitchen and could not help but hear. If you accept this offer, I wish I would have let you die of gangrene."

"I don't understand. Is it because of his offer of Rosamond?"

Elsie scoffed. The once pretty face was now a mask of bitterness. "I've grown to hate the slave trade and this life. I care not what we may have lost, but I will not lose my daughter to a man with blood on his hands."

Preacher could now understand her coldness to him, but realized no amount of explanation would change her opinion.

It was a miserable dinner. Michael Langhorne, while Preacher washed, had received a message from Collin Young. Thoroughout the meal he sat slumped in his chair as though he had lost all his roots. Elsie Langhorne picked at her food with disinterest. Rosamond Langhorne ravished everything in sight, as though she had been starved for weeks. Preacher's non-interest in his food was due only in part to his conversations with Michael and Elsie.

He couldn't concentrate on his plate for looking at Rosamond. Seven months had made a drastic change in the sixteen year old. What had been flat was now a fully budding breast. The straight line form had been molded into an hourglass gown. Little girl curls were now a young lady's crown. A saucy face was now ravishing. Preacher was enraptured. Seeing her in this light made her father's offer more desirable.

The odd note came when the stablemaster came to report on the broken wheel of his surrey. Michael brushed it aside with an invitation to stay the night. Elsie used it as an excuse to go and fix him a proper room. Rosamond yawned, said her goodnights and gave Preacher a knowing wink.

Preacher felt like he was being set up, just like in the bar. A wheel from a Langhorne Oak surrey could have been used to fix the broken one, or Elsie could have offered one of their many riding horses. And Langhorne Oaks had ample guest rooms which were always made up and ready. Preacher steeled himself for a reopening of Michael's offer.

To his surprise, the old man began to ramble on about his favorite topic—himself and the proud family line of the Langhornes. The subject matter became disjointed and he fell asleep in the middle of a sentence.

Preacher slipped away and ambled toward the atrium at the rear of the huge house. Deep in the shadows of the climbing rose bushes he found Rosamond.

"I wondered if you would recall that this was my favorite spot to come of a summer evening."

Preacher laughed. It was the sound of his youth returned. "I had to wait until your father fell asleep in the middle of one of his stories."

She turned away, as though that could lead into a conversation she did not want to discuss. "Come, let's walk out through the garden."

"No," Preacher said, "the night is turning chilly. It's autumn and not summer. Let's stay here."

"As you wish." She stared toward the wrought iron benches at the open end of the atrium. The rising moon was casting the garden in silver. "Last week we gathered mistletoe and hung it in the garden trees to dry for Christmas. Of course, if you had a mind to, you could pretend that I hung it here in the atrium."

Preacher looked at her and a hard glint appeared in his brown eyes. For a moment she had sounded as coy and playful as JenaBelle Trotter. He put JenaBelle out of his mind. Rosamond had been his first kiss, soft and clinging with a quiet demand. If this was her subtle invitation to take up where they had left off, he was up to the challenge. He pulled her up from the bench and took her into his strong arms. In seven months, and several female teachers later, he knew the power of a male kiss to stir the ardor of female passion.

But it was Preacher, again, who broke away from the embrace.

"You are growing up," he panted.

She laughed throatily and dangerously. "See what you have been missing by being in Missouri? Have I been learning well?"

"Too damn well! Who has been teaching you?"

"I didn't ask who has been teaching you, James David."

She leaned forward again, this time taking his hand and placing it gently on the cup of her breast.

"Rosamond!" he gasped.

Her whisper was seductive. "I've known you wanted your hand there ever since I helped nurse you back to health from Jamie Fuller's bullet wound."

"Wanting," he stammered, "and doing, are two different things."

Daringly, she rubbed his hand over the cloth until he could feel her nipple stiffen and harden.

The heat rose around Preacher's neck and beat about his face in waves. Not even a professional, like Jean-Luc, had aroused him to such hardness. And oddly, the memory of that marvelous female put Rosamond back into her true Southern tradition spot.

"No," he said miserably, "we're forgetting who and what we are."

"Man talk," she said gravely. "You certainly forgot who you were, and what you were, with Betsy Fuller!"

"I never kissed her," he said.

"That's not what put her with child!" she snapped. Then she softened. "I'm not pointing the finger of blame, James David. Reggie told me about Zachary, himself, and Collin Young. She played with fire and got burned."

"And you don't think we would be playing with fire?"

"Different fire. I heard what my father said to you, even though it turned my mother livid. Mama hasn't found the man she thinks is suitable for me. That's why she sent her own cousin, Randolph Newberry, packing back to Atlanta. He is really quite a man, but Mama felt he was developing into more than just a kissing cousin. I wish she could see that someday you could become man enough for me.''

Someday? Preacher felt affronted, even angry. He had been man enough for Morgana Lake and JenaBelle Trotter in Missouri.

Neither saw the rider come through the shadows of the garden fruit trees, pass within ten feet of the open end of the atrium, and head for the front of the mansion.

Preacher's only concern was to prove his manly status to Rosamond. He took her fully into his arms, and his hands explored her breasts until the covering cotton cloth was moist and clinging.

"Not here," she panted. "Mama has put you in your old sick room. I know how to get there without her hearing me."

"You go in first. I have to cool down a bit."

"Don't cool down too much," she giggled and ran for the house.

Michael Langhorne stood in the foyer, leaning heavily on his cane. Little men were again messing into his master scheme and now his daughter had his ire rising.

"What is the meaning of this?" he demanded, as Rosamond came along the hall from the atrium.

"Meaning?"

"Your wanton behavior with James David in the atrium!"

"Who told you that?" she demanded hotly.

"There is a full moon, young lady, and Mack McDuffy could see you both quite plainly. Where is James David?"

Rosamond looked startled. She was unused to hearing such an angry tone in her father's voice. She knew McDuffy must have seen all, but why report to her father? McDuffy was secretly paid by her mother to keep Collin Young and the federal troops away from Langhorne Oaks. But, as she had learned from age three and upward, she could get around her father. "James David? He will be in shortly. It was time for bed."

"Well," Michael sighed with relief, "at least you came to your senses before real damage was done."

"Done? What did Mr. McDuffy report to you, with his evil

little mind, and why is he here at this hour of the night."

"That is none of your damn business," a voice growled from the study door.

Michael Langhorne felt like slapping his daughter, but his frustration was really with McDuffy. The man had demanded to see Mrs. Langhorne, as though Michael were no longer master. For the moment his mind drifted. Rosamond saw and took charge.

"If you enter our house," she said, on an overly sweet note, "then it becomes my business, Mr. McDuffy."

"Not really," he said candidly. "Collin Young sent a message to your mother and father that I would be here as his deputy sheriff. The Preacher kid shot Jerry Donner this afternoon. Your parents said they would not interefere when I came to arrest him."

Rosamond back stiffened. Her voice dropped to a spiteful crispness.

"I was in Lungstrum's General Store, Mr. McDuffy!" she breathed, her wrath growing by the moment. "Captain Kelley came in and reported to the ladies present what the shooting had been about. James David was not arrested then, so why now?"

Mack McDuffy didn't answer her. He stood very still and his mouth tightened into a hard line. He and Collin Young knew the true facts, but they didn't matter. Collin Young wanted James David six feet under ground because of Betsy Fuller. McDuffy wanted him taken care of because of the embarrassment he suffered at the duel. But McDuffy had learned his lesson in going against James David alone. This time he had six of Donner's friends lying in ambush down the road.

The front door started to swing in. McDuffy took no chance. He whipped out his sidearm and pounded six slugs into the oak panel. Rosamond screamed and screamed again. There was no cry of pain or thud of dead body. That lack was infinitely worse than her screams.

Then, ever so slowly, the door swung open again. Preacher stood there grinning, smoothing his hand down the outside panel.

"Too thick to penetrate, McDuffy, and I can have fists on

you before you can reload. What's your game?''

''To arrest you,'' he said simply and without charge or reason.

''You'll make a fool of yourself, if it is over Jerry Donner. Captain Kelley will have me sprung by morning.''

''But you will belong to Collin and me until morning.'' Then he paled, realizing he was without ammunition in his weapon and no match for the brawn of Preacher. ''Why don't you just come along, peaceful like.''

Preacher saw his problem and faced one of his own. He was the only one in a position to see Elsie Langhorne standing at the top of the stairs. He would not cause the woman embarrassment in her own house by causing trouble.

''Let's go,'' he gruffed at McDuffy and marched out the door.

Elsie swept down the stairs and into the study. Michael came out of his reverie as Elsie came out of the study and thrust a rifle and pistol into Rosamond's hands.

''What are you doing?'' Michael demanded.

''She is going to ride and help James David. If not, Rosamond, ride to warn Captain Kelley of this arrest.''

Michael looked foolishly at his wife. ''What is this? You knew from the note that McDuffy was coming for him.''

''You've become a horrible liar, Michael Patrick Langhorne,'' she said grimly. ''Rosamond, I fear your father is a very sick man. I knew nothing of this, and am most angry at Mr. McDuffy for not informing me. James David's horse and surrey are still rigged behind the barn. There was never anything wrong with it in the first place. Go, before we have blood on our hands.''

Michael started to protest, but the look on his wife's face told him that it would be a losing battle. Then, just as suddenly, he forgot what the battle was all about and ambled back into his study and to the brandy bottle.

Mother and daughter locked eyes and did not speak. Rosamond turned and raced from the house, a world of questions swarming in her brain.

Mack McDuffy began to fret over his assignment before he had Preacher halfway down the Langhorne Oaks entry road.

It had been too easy. Preacher had even stood calmly while he had reloaded his pistol. Something had to be wrong. He had expected Elsie Langhorne to be there and handle her senile husband. He smelled trouble, just like he smelled it the foggy morning of the duel.

"How did Young know I'd be at the Langhorne plantation?" Preacher asked.

"Never you mind," McDuffy growled. "Just keep that damn horse in front of mine and your hands on the saddle-horn."

"Quite a horse you are on, Mack. Recognize it as one of my mother's stock. When did Collin start paying you enough to buy a Bradburn Hill steed?"

"Weren't stolen, if that's what you mean! Was a gift for favor done."

"Like the favor of learning where I was this evening? Seems to me I saw my brother riding that horse no less than two weeks ago."

McDuffy pushed his battered hat to the back of his head and urged his horse to come abreast of Preacher's. He saw no reason to let the kid know that Elsie Langhorne had bought the horse for him two weeks ago, but did see reason to give Preacher a few grains of truth about his brother before the ambush gunned him down.

"You goddam Preacher people make me sick. You get away with murder after murder. Your Ma sells more horses north than she does south. Your Pa makes you and your brother out to be saints, but Zach Preacher ain't no fuckin' saint, buddy-boy. He was so hot to get into your houseguest's pants that he told me quick you were visiting Langhorne Oaks. Thought that funny, thinking that filly was your gal, till I saw you kissin' Miss Rosamond 'n feeling her titties. Never thought you had stuck Betsy Fuller till I saw you in action tonight. Then—" he stopped short and turned.

A surrey was racing down the plantation entry road, the horse at a whipped full gallop. McDuffy was confused. Only one woman in these parts could handle a surrey at such breakneck speed—Elsie Langhorne. Was he to wait for further orders from her?

For once McDuffy thought on his own. He would soon be near the point of the ambush. It might serve his purpose with Captain Kelley to have an eye witness to his survival of the attack. He urged his horse forward.

Preacher gave a grimace of disgust on hearing and then seeing the chasing surrey. That it was his surrey was a bit of amazement, but what the fool was up to he could not fathom. When McDuffy urged the horses forward, Preacher let his horse follow, matching McDuffy's. For a quarter-of-a-mile McDuffy didn't seem to care that the surrey was closing ground. They came to the big bend in the road, with hickory stands to each side. It was like a long dark tunnel with the moonlight not penetrating.

Suddenly McDuffy spurred his horse into a full gallop as he rounded the bend. The long legs of the Bradburn Hill steed put immediate distance between them. Preacher sensed something unusual and beat his horse to match the gallop and try to pull abreast. Rounding the bend he could see the end of the dark tunnel and saw a group of horsemen sitting in full moonlight. A dark suspicion began forming in his mind as he spurred the horse to even more speed. Weaponless, he had to use McDuffy as a protective shield.

McDuffy did not want Preacher near to him. He turned his horse left and right to keep Preacher from coming abreast. Preacher had wanted to get to McDuffy's left side and a possible chance of reaching over to steal his gun. McDuffy began to sense the same and moved his horse to the left shoulder of the road. That left his ride side open for Preacher to move up inch by inch. McDuffy used the end of his reins to lash at the head of Preacher's horse. It angered the horse to move forward away from the blows rather than retreat. It also caused McDuffy to concentrate on Preacher's horse and not Preacher. They were now abreast, the horses bumping each other for space as the road narrowed. Ahead, the horsemen were beginning to form a wall of horses and drawn weapons.

Preacher froze his left hand and let his arm swing forward and back with a well aimed blow. With all his weight behind the swing, and McDuffy surging forward, the edge of his hand ate into McDuffy's Adam's Apple. The cry was caught in the man's throat. He sailed backwards out of the saddle and began to roll in the dirt like a windblown tumbleweed.

Seeing what had transpired, four of the horsemen began to charge but Preacher paid them no mind. He jumped from his galloping horse and let the animal surge forward. Preacher rolled into the ground, gained his footing and ran to the gasping McDuffy. The man did not resist as Preacher took his gun, his fear more centered on not being able to get enough air.

The horsemen were nearly upon Preacher when he was able to turn and start firing the weapon. It was an old weapon with a faulty trajectory. Six shots and only one minor scream of pain. Worse still, the ground around him was starting to jump from their fired bullets. He dove into the underbrush just as he heard the crack of a rifle. A horseman screamed his last cry and fell some twenty feet from Preacher.

The rifle shot had come from the surrey. Preacher had the choice of racing for the dead man's guns or running for the surrey, which was making the other horsemen scatter and turn.

Preacher measured the charge of the surrey and ran for it. Oddly, he was surprised to find that the madwoman with reins in one hand and rifle in the other was Rosamond.

He swung into the back seat and yelled, "Give me that pea shooter and keep the horse at full gallop!"

Rosamond brought the whip down on the horse's flanks. The surrey careened down the country road toward the other horsemen. Preacher crouched and rested the rifle on the back surrey seat. The other horsemen were turning again to pursue the surrey. Preacher took careful aim at a large rider and fired. The man continued to charge and return the fire.

"Damn!" Preacher cursed. "Aim's no better than McDuffy's pistol."

This time he aimed for the man's belly button and fired with the same results. He picked up the spent cartridge and cursed again.

"Keep your head down!" he yelled. "This is loaded with blanks and they aim to kill us!"

Rosamond laughed to herself with amused contempt. Her

mother did all the reloading of cartridges at Langhorne Oaks
and it was her mother who had given her the rifle and pistol.

"The pistol will be the same," she called. "Crawl up
front."

Even as Preacher began to follow her direction, she took
another pistol from her lap and fired at the men ahead. The
men turned to get out of her range. They had been told that
Preacher would be unarmed and unaided.

"Mother didn't know I brought along father's favorite
pistol." She handed it to him for reloading. "You might
notice that the ones behind us are all quite alive and checking
on Mr. McDuffy."

Preacher turned back. The man who had cried his last was
up and tending to the deputy sheriff. The other three were
getting down from the horses and not pursuing. He realized
she had made the statement without looking back.

"How did you know that?"

She ignored him. The horsemen ahead of them were
rounding the next bend. She kept the horse straight ahead
toward the underbrush. It shied, but she whipped it forward
and it gently broke through the tangle to a well concealed,
seldom used road. She let the frightened horse slow to a trot.

"What in the hell is this all about?" Preacher screamed.

"Survival," Rosamond said coolly. "I heard father set up
this meeting with you this morning. I understood it was to be
a peace meeting between you and Collin Young. That, of
course, was before the Jerry Donner affair. I thought things
had changed when I heard you were to stay the night."

"Your father didn't mean a word he said, did he?"

She turned and laughed, seeing the expression of wonder
on his face.

"Mother fights to keep it a family secret, James David. My
father doesn't mean anything he says anymore."

That statement was supposed to explain everything, but
Preacher's look demanded more.

"When news came that Charles Barrington had killed you,
my brother accused my father of murder and left for the war.
He has not been the same since. We didn't even know he was
involved in that silly duel until he came home wounded.

Mother, of course, blames you for everything.''

"Did she know about tonight?"

"On that point I am somewhat confused. I know she has been paying McDuffy to keep the federal troops away from the plantation, but she did seem surprised at McDuffy being there tonight.''

Preacher frowned. "I can't understand your father giving you guns loaded with blanks. You could have been killed. Where are we going?"

"You said it was better on a bed," she laughed.

"I was talking about your bed at the plantation, and a saner moment than this.''

"This is also my bed," she said coolly, bringing the horse to a walk. "It is a private cabin I had built so I could sometimes get away on my own. The county has become hateful to us, James David. No more party invitations. We don't even give parties anymore. Mother was forced to cancel the barbecue. Folks who used to laugh and dance together now hate each other. I'm sick of this spiteful old war.''

She began to turn the horse into a rutted lane. "You jump off here and make sure that we aren't being followed. You'll find cut branches to hide our turn in.''

Obediently, Preacher got down and listened. There was no sound of hoof beats anywhere nearby. He was still puzzled over the entire matter and her lack of knowledge on some points. He found the cut branches and puzzled even more. They were fresh cut, as early as that afternoon. He turned. The surrey was disappearing into the dense shadows of the hickory grove. Then, he heard the slow, tracking hoofbeats of a horse coming along. He moved into the tangle of the undergrowth, away from the cut branches, and peered out. It took a minute for the horse to come abreast of his position. There was no mistaking the stern, bitter countenance of Collin Young. He waited for Collin to ride up the little country trek and then back. The cut branches were fresh enough that Collin did not see the difference, and the dry autumn road was packed enough so that the wheel tracks did not show. Still, he waited another fifteen minutes and then went to find the surrey hidden in the grove.

Ten feet beyond the surrey he found a small clearing with an eight foot by eight foot split log shack. It reminded him of the playhouse his father had once made for Abigail. The floor was pounded earth, holding upon its surface little more than a cot bed and a small table and chair. A single lantern and flint box were the only ornaments on the table and the chair was now covered with Rosamond's discarded clothing. Upon hearing his entrance, she reached out from beneath the coverlet and turned down the lantern wick.

The open door still spotlighted the bed in a shaft of moonlight. She lay on her back, eyes closed, arms ramrod over her head with clenched fists.

Preacher could not help but laugh. "Why are you suddenly so fearful?"

"Our negro mammy says this is the way white virgin girls are supposed to act."

Now he did roar with mirth as he quickly undressed. "After the way you were kissing, girl, you are greatly overacting."

She made a rude sound and let her fists unclench. With one quick movement he swept the coverlet from her nude form and onto the floor. He stood and marveled at what he had always longed to see. The golden hair cascaded over her shoulders and rested on perfectly molded young breasts with pouting nipples. He saw the flat stomach slightly tremble with anticipation. His eyes rested on the golden curls hiding the treasure that would now be his and his alone.

He climbed between the soft, feminine legs, positioned himself and gently let his length move through the hairy mound and find a moist entrance. There was no cry of pain, no denial of his right to be penetrating, no breaking of a virginal shield. Preacher felt his length slide effortlessly deeper and deeper without a wince, or a cry of pleasure or pain. Even a girl like Betsy Fuller had been enamored over the marvelous male size of his penis. Every woman he had known, which was now four, had built his ego over the fact of his uncommon size. Rosamond's non-response was deflating his ego, but not his desire.

Expertly taught, he settled into a sensual pumping motion,

using his powerful thighs to spread her legs further apart and allow more and more of his mighty organ to drop into the smooth vagina. But there was no response, no tightness, no interest in becoming a combining partner.

The thought came cold and crisp to his mind. Everyone seemed to want to play with the mind and body of James David Preacher as though he were still a naive little boy. Others might think they could use them in their power struggle, but no woman was going to make a fool of him in bed.

"Who was he?" he growled hotly in her ear. Rosamond stiffened, but did not answer. He pulled himself forward and let her taste for the first time the true measure of his length. This time she did gasp, but out of anger at his animal like lunge.

"You're no virgin!" he declared. "Tell me who took you first!"

"You," she said indifferently, "as far as the county and Mama are concerned."

"Damn them all to hell!" he snorted. "Who beat me to you, Rosamond?"

"No one!" she snapped. "I can go to my grave saying you were the only man I knew."

"Tell me! Tell me! Tell me!" he gasped, his anger and urge building at an equal pitch.

She refused to answer, but could not refuse to cooperate as her own urge mounted. But she had been too late in joining the game and making it a combined pleasure. She had let him surge too far ahead, so that when he shuddered on a commanding thrust, she, only then began to demand her own fulfillment. A fulfillment he could not sate as he withdrew, angry, frustrated and put upon.

"Do you always leave your other women hanging?" she asked smugly.

"Only an experienced woman would know that fact," he sneered, rising to dress.

She yawned and stretched. "You are a country bumpkin, James David. I wish you were more of a gentleman, like my Cousin Randolph. He makes a woman really feel like she is a woman.''

Preacher's face purpled at the comparsion and then he read into it a glimmer of truth.

''If you are trying to make me believe it was your mother's cousin, then why play this silly virgin game with me?''

She climbed from the cot and started to dress, the pale oval of her face filled with maddening serenity.

''Would you have had me, otherwise?'' she said, coolly. ''I think not. Still, you are the only game in town. Mother thinks that she hates you, but I can change her tune if she feels you have taken my mind off Randolph.''

''You all have gone mad!''

He stopped short. Something in the way she had said Randolph's name disturbed him. He straightened, looming up before her so tall that his head almost touched the cabin ceiling.

''I learned quite a lot out West, Rosamond. The tone of voice gives a liar away. You lied to me. Randolph may be a gentleman, but I doubt he was the one to bed you. Name me that man!''

She stood quite still before him, her blue eyes widening in her white face. Then, very softly, she began to laugh. ''I won't name names, James David, because it is a Langhorne family matter and does not concern you.''

It was like a slap in the face. He cringed at the truth he suspected. The only male Langhorne in her age group would be Reggie Langhorne. He refused to believe it.

She was quickly dressed and at the door.

''You will be safe here tonight,'' she said, as though nothing else had transpired. ''I'll sneak back in the morning with breakfast. No one knows about this cabin but Reggie and me. He built it for me last year when we feared we might have a slave rebellion. We spent many nights here, safe from that terror.''

She turned and fled to the surrey. Preacher silently watched her go, not wishing any further information. His mind was in a fog. He waited for the sound of the surrey to fade and then he stepped out into the night air and started walking. He couldn't spend another moment in that cabin and in no way did he want to return to Langhorne Oaks. Like a wounded animal, he just wanted to crawl to a safe place and lick his wounds.

Chapter 5

IT WAS NEAR midnight when he got home to a house of mourning and confusion. He didn't get a chance to lick his wounds.

His mother, Morgana and Mama Dee, once over their shock at seeing him alive, all tried to talk at once. Preacher pushed aside his melancholy remorse and took forceful charge.

"Mama, go break the news gently to father. Mama Dee, make a lot of black coffee, it will be a long night. Morgana, what time did Collin Young bring the news to Zachary?"

Morgana was still shaking from having been pulled from the pit of deep grief to the joy of seeing him alive.

"We had just finished supper, almost six-thirty. The full moon was just rising. Mama Dee wailed that bad news always comes on a full moon night." She gulped. "He said that Mac McDuffy, on his way to Langhorne Oakes, was a moment too late to stop an ambush by some of Jerry Donner's friends."

"An' we been awaitin' dem ta bring back yore body," Mama Dee got in.

Preacher grinned. "Collin jumped the gun on his plan. At that time Mack was just getting to Langhorne Oakes to arrest me. Now I know why Collin was snooping around. He still needed a dead body to bring back."

"Mas'sa James David!" Mama Dee cried. "Ya'all get yourself 'way frum dat window. You a good target in de lamp light, if'n he lookin' ta hab you dead!"

"She's right," Morgana frowned. "Mama Dee, bring the

coffee into the little parlor. Its heavy drapes won't allow light to show through."

"Jeremy," she said quietly when they were in the hallway, "you came in upset, even before you got this news. Were the Langhorne people involved?"

He shrugged. "I could say yes and I could say no. I didn't know Michael Langhorne was going looney. They all seem a little looney to me, after tonight."

"Including Rosamond?"

"Yes," he said gruffly. "She's no longer mine, Morgana. She tried to make me think she had known Mrs. Langhorne's Cousin Randolph, but I have a horrible feeling that she learned of life from her brother Reggie."

"That wouldn't surprise me, from what Zach told me about him tonight."

He turned, amazed. "Zach told you things about Reggie?"

She entered the little parlor. It was lit only by the dying embers from the fireplace. "Jeremy, before supper Zach opened up to me like a book needing cleansing. I learned more about him in an hour than you have in sixteen years. He confessed all of his sins to me."

There was a silence between them. It seemed to last for an eternity until he could stand it no longer. He turned, his hands shooting out, grabbing her thin shoulders.

"Morgana!" he croaked, his voice strangling. "He told Mack McDuffy I was at Langhorne Oaks. He knew I was to be ambushed this evening!"

"Who told you such clap-trap? It's rubbish! Zach was with me from the moment you left us until the moment that Collin Young arrived. He was as shocked over your reported death as the rest of us. For my sake, don't make bad blood where there is none."

"For your sake?"

She took his hands and folded them under her chin. "Jeremy, you and I are family. I've had a growing interest in Zach since my arrival, but he never noticed me until today. You and your problems with Zach stood in the way. This evening we were able to talk, man to woman."

"Man to woman?" he scoffed. "Morgana, he'll break your heart."

"You know me better than that, Jeremy James David Preacher. No man gets the best of me."

"Do you love him?" he asked, then was furious with himself for having asked the question, recognizing in it the beginning of defeat.

"I do," she said softly, "with a heart that can sympathize with his little boy actions, and with a mind that can understand—"

"Understand what?" he growled.

"The stupid, pitiful and mean things that he has pulled on you for sixteen years out of jealousy and fear that he was unwanted and unloved. No, he has not been a good or a nice brother, but when you were reported dead he took full blame. He admitted to your mother and me how he had set up and egged you into the shootout with Jerry Donner. He knew you would be alive if he had not pulled that stunt. Jeremy, you are the boy who has become a full man. He is not yet a full man. He's in your father's study. Let him know that you are still alive."

"Damn!" he croaked. "I'll do it, but only for your sake."

He pushed open the door of his father's study. The bay window cast the room in moonlight. Zachary sat by the unlit fireplace, his back to the door, a corn liquor jug in one hand and a glass in the other. Each swallow was bitter with the taste of grief and guilt.

Preacher tiptoed around the chair and stood there staring down at Zach's stark face. He could have killed him at that moment with his bare hands, but he suddenly felt no rage. Instead, he oddly felt a surge of great pity. At sixteen he knew the evil and savage acts that men played upon their fellow men. Zach, he realized would have to learn to live with his guilt.

"Zach," he said softly. "Zach—"

Zachary looked up. The jug and glass crashed to the floor as though a ghost had suddenly materialized.

"James David?" he stammered and rose up. Then, he realized this was no apparition and he crushed his brother in a great embrace and his bloodshot, whiskey hazed eyes filled with real tears.

"Does Pa know?" he wailed.

"Mother is with him. I'll go up in a minute."

"I want you to know—"

"No!" he roared, breaking from the embrace as though it were disgusting him. "I wish no words from your mouth. Now or ever! And these are the only words I shall utter to you! Morgana seems to have an interest in you, God help her. She is a lady and like a sister to me. Treat her badly and I will call you out."

He turned and marched from the room.

Matilda Preacher was no fool. She let her son ramble on, telling the events of the evening. The firebrand Irish woman saw the situation as little different than in the raising of one of her thoroughbred horses. A youthful mare could always find a way of luring a stud horse into the wrong pasture.

"I don't like it! I just don't like it," she finally exclaimed. "Rosamond is making herself out to be your rescuing heroine, which strikes me as right odd. Why leave you in that cabin for the night?"

"So there would be no murder on the plantation proper!"

They turned as one to the open bedroom door. Captain Andrew Kelley stood there, his face the picture of malicious glee. No one questioned his charge.

"I thought only people in the Bible rose from the dead, James David," he chuckled.

"How did you know I was reported dead?"

"Collin Young's boast at Hartley's Tavern," he mocked. "Claimed you had been ambushed and that Mack McDuffy had the situation under control. I let him think I had no interest in the matter and rode out the back way to the Langhorne plantation. Funny, all I saw was some men bringing McDuffy back to town clutching his throat. I didn't let them see me, but I didn't see your dead body, either. Then, I nearly got run down by Miss Langhorne, driving a surrey like the devil was on her tail. She claims you tried to rape her and she stole the surrey to get away."

"Didn't happen like that," Preacher said, flat and expressionless.

"Struck me that way too, boy. The lady had a pistol in her lap and two more weapons in the surrey. Rape, or attempted rape, seems strange with such firepower. Nor did she ask me to see her home safely, or demand that I go thrash you to save her honor. Took me a spell to find the cabin. It was deserted. Right curious. Collin saying you were dead, she claiming rape—but no you. Except, you almost got me killed."

"What do you mean?"

"I no sooner was in the cabin than I heard men coming through the woods. They opened fire as soon as they saw the cabin. Young called out to you, claiming you were weaponless, so surrender or die. I fired in the direction of the voice and he screamed out. Before they could react I unloaded both guns, crawled away into the woods and back to where I had my horse hidden. Got back onto the plantation road and waited for them to come along."

"That's odd," Preacher mused. "Young was trying to find his way to the cabin earlier. Doesn't sound like he just stumbled on it, like you."

"He didn't, and you won't like my answer. His men brought him along with a shattered leg and a change of tune. Seems you thwarted an arrest and ambush by kidnapping Miss Langhorne. Elsie Langhorne told them where you were hiding and demanded your arrest. He was quick to shove that job back upon me."

"And here you are," Preacher said wearily. "Damn, those people can lie right on top of a lie. I'll never be safe from them or Collin Young."

"Reckon you can be packed to ride within the half-hour?" Kelly asked.

"Packed? Ride to where?"

"Army headquarters in Virginia. I need to get a message to the authorities to replace Young with full military authority for this area."

"How is that going to help?" Matilda demanded. "They'll just start hounding him again on his return."

"That might be a spell, Mrs. Preacher. If I let him go, I'll expect him to stay there for the turkey shoot. The war is heating up in that area.''

Preacher stared at the officer in sudden puzzlement. ''Why am I always forced to run from things that I didn't do?''

''Thunderation!'' Daniel Preacher boomed, sitting straight up in his bed. ''The man is trying to save your life! We are hated enough for your actions of the past and Elsie Langhorne can be a she-devil. She'll make every hussy in the county believe the rape charge and nothing Captain Kelley says will change their minds. He asked you kindly, but I am ordering. Matilda, get out that rifle and pistol that I bought in San Antonio. They were used at the Alamo and are proper war weapons. You will leave your other weapons behind. You are going to war and not a gunfight!''

''What of Zachary?'' Matilda asked.

''He stays home,'' Daniel snapped. ''Can't send two off to war. Might as well send the one who has the taste of killing in him. I've said all I am going to say on the matter!''

Preacher knew there was no chance to rebel. He also knew that from that moment on there would be a silence, a gulf, a chasm between he and his father. His actions that night made it impossible for him to stay and help manage the plantation. To Daniel Preacher's disgust, he would have to put Zachary in the role and the blame would fall back on James David's shoulders. Zachary was going to win by default.

Preacher was ready within the half-hour. When he said goodbye to his father the old man locked his lips in silence. He intentionally did not say goodbye to Zach, but was covered with hugs and kisses from Morgana and Abigail. Only Matilda Preacher remained strong and tearless.

''This is Thor, my son. I named him after a war god because I knew that it would be his destiny to go to war. I did not know that he would carry one of my sons, but he is an intelligent and well trained piece of horse flesh. I, also, repacked your saddlebags. I don't want you leaving Barrington's weapons here, and your father is a romantic. Weapons that fought at the Alamo are a little ancient for this modern battle.''

Captain Kelley approached and gave the report he had

been writing out in Daniel Preacher's study.

Preacher read the front of the envelope and shook his head. "Why did you say that your messenger is J.D. Preacher?"

"Irony," Kelley mocked. "You told me how Betsy Fuller was the first to call you J.D. Well, when Collin smells out what I have done, he'll have the Army looking for a James David Preacher. We are not well organized with paperwork. They'll never find you. If you are ready, I'll ride along with you."

"I'd rather ride alone."

Kelley nodded and watched him effortlessly mount the beautiful black beast. They made a massive, impressive pair. The midnight black horse and a rider whose mother had dressed him all in black so he would blend into the safety of the night.

It was a ruse that worked well. Halfway down the circular drive a cloud scudded across the moon. When it passed, he had vanished from sight.

Preacher had entered the woods, taking a little used trail that would by-pass the little community, as well as farm and plantation houses. The trail headed due east. He sat tall in the saddle, pulled erect by that thing which had pulled him from boyhood to manhood in such a short span of time. He was a Preacher. Bred into him was Matilda's Irish daring, fire and determination to face all danger squarely. Likewise, stamped irrevocably and ineradicably upon the very stuff of his being, was the cold, callous, even-thinking temper of his English father.

Once again James David Preacher, the boy, was being left behind. Riding forth was J.D. Preacher, the man. He would never be able to look back, because his youth was now like chaff in the wind.

CHAPTER 6

PREACHER LISTENED TO the gentleman soldier's carping. He was blunt in his response. "Of course I know how to shoot. I was trained for the Missouri Militia by Morgan Lake. It may hurt your sensitive ears, but those men are born knowing how to handle a weapon."

"Get that braggin' little bastard out of my unit!"

Colonel Taylor Wagner laughed delightedly. "If his weapon knowledge is proving to be an embarrassment, make him a training officer."

"No! He is too damn young!"

Wagner relented and moved Preacher to another unit. Here, among a group of mainly farmers, Preacher found better marksmen, but a different resentment. His mount and weapon were superior to set him apart. For three frustrating months he was shuffled about, gaining the reputation of a malcontent miscast.

"Jesus!" Reggie Langhorne cried triumphantly, "what a treat to see a face from home!"

Preacher hardly recognized the man in the resplendant uniform of a Major. Once prone to be overweight, Reggie now seemed lean and muscular. Preacher started to smile at the warm greeting and then remembrance took the smile away.

"If you're my new Commanding Officer," Preacher mused, "I reckon you and me can't serve together."

"Oh, forget it, James David," Reggie snapped. "What your brother and I did was a local matter, we now have a war to fight."

"War to fight," Preacher repeated, "is why I was sent here. I can't serve under a man who is a liar, a cheat and a user of women. Yeah, I learned about Rosamond."

"Mind your manners," Reggie barked, and quickly looked around to make sure he was surrounded by loyal officers and soldiers. He was aware of Preacher's gunfighting reputation and did not want a personal showdown. "You are an infantry soldier in the Confederate States of America army and will respect my officer's rank."

Preacher stared at him with sober hate.

"I respect the rank," he said flatly, "but I cannot respect, or serve under, a man who would take his own sister to his bed for pleasure!"

Reggie reeled, as though Preacher had given him a stinging slap to the jaw.

"Lie!" he roared. "Who filled your ears with such trash?"

"Rosamond. She took me to that cabin you built for her."

A young officer chuckled.

Langhorne glared him to silence. He was a patient and well-trained officer, immediately recognizing that no amount of words would change Preacher's mind on this personal family matter.

"James David," he reasoned, "you are most correct that we cannot serve together." A slow, knowing smile lighted his eyes. "Private Hanson, escort Private Preacher and his records to Infantry Company F. I feel that Commanding Officer will be able to handle this hothead and his daring charges."

Preacher started to protest, but Reggie Langhorne had turned his back on him and the sentry brought his rifle to the ready, as though Preacher were a prisoner. It was another frustration, but he felt he had unnerved Reggie with the charge.

Moments later he had to rethink that thought. The tents of the two companies nearly joined. He was stunned when the sentry presented his records to Major Randolph Newberry. He had a chance to measure the man while his record was quietly studied.

Randolph Newberry was not what Preacher had expected. He was still a remarkably youthful man at age 39. Tall, lean and Nordic handsome. He was respected by his troops for his intelligent genius, quick and daring command decisions. They had already seen battle duty and were in camp to replenish their losses.

Preacher saw at once his error. Reggie had put him under the command of the man who knew the vital truth about Rosamond. Preacher cursed his stupidity. He could see at once how Rosamond might have fallen into passion over this blond god.

"I don't like your past record," Newberry scowled. "Have you a reason why my Cousin Reginald would not accept you as a recruit?"

A warning light in Preacher's brain flashed a caution signal. The man had a new and fashionable weapon, which he wore as a professional. He was wearing the ancient piece given to him by his father, his own in the saddlebag. He had to be careful before he charged the man.

"Family matter, sir," he said calmly. "Our family plantations are but eight miles distant."

"Of course," Newberry chuckled. "Thought I recognized the Preacher name. That would be Bradburn Hill. I've spent time in Tennessee at my Cousin Elsie's plantation. Do you know her daughter Rosamond?"

"I do sir, since childhood."

Newberry winked. "And how was that lovely Miss Rosamond when you left home?"

"About ready to be given to me in marriage," Preacher grinned and then hardened his eyes to cold challenge, "until I learned she was no longer virginal. Seems she still pines for you and that secret cabin in the woods."

Newberry blinked and tried to ignore the chuckle that came from the sentry who had heard this charge before. Had the youth been an officer, the words would have demanded an immediate duel. But, Randolph Newberry prided himself on his sophistication and power in frightening people to bow to his demands. He thought he saw a weakness in this recruit that he could exploit and still his knowledge about Rosamond Langhorne. He walked to the recruit's handsome horse and looked at Thor with covetous greed.

"Private," he sneered, "we are basically an infantry company. Only officers are allowed to have a horse. And, as you are not an officer, or hardly officer material, your mount, as of this moment, is the property of this company and its Commanding Officer.''

"You touch my horse and you are dead!"

Newberry laughed with devilish delight. With a smoothness that reminded Preacher of Charles Barrington, he drew his weapon from a highly polished leather sheath and fired over Thor's head at a Virginia pine tree. A pine cone shattered and the sky filled with frightened birds.

Neither Preacher nor Thor flinched. Newberry was impressed and knew he faced a challenge.

"The beast is well trained to warfare noise, but can he take this?"

Again he fired, splintering the top of the pine tree to shreds.

"How?" Preacher gasped.

Newberry smiled sweetly. He loved to boast about his LeMat and make other men covet his possession.

"The how of it, you young whippersnapper, is that the LeMat fires ten shots with two barrels, the upper one being a grapeshot 18 gauge shotgun."

Preacher was enthralled. "Where might one purchase such a piece?"

Preacher was eyed as though he were one of the poor white farmer soldiers. The Southern aristrocrat's words dripped with venom. "There are only a half-dozen of them in America, made only for gentlemen, of course. Now, as I still have eight shots left in the chamber, stand aside so I may test my new horse."

Preacher backed away, but not out of fear of the LeMat. Randolph sheathed the gun and took the reins. He had one foot in the stirrup when Reggie came running over from his tent.

"Cousin Randolph!" he cried. "That's a Matilda Preacher trained horse!"

"Of that, I am quite aware," he laughed, swinging up into the English saddle.

Thor allowed the officer to settle into the saddle. Randolph Newberry sat straight and proud. He could feel the power of the beast beneath him and it increased his arrogant pride to think the beast was now his. He touched his heels to the horse's flanks and flipped the reins to begin his parade. Then he gasped. To his utter surprise the horse had not started to prance forward, but from a standing position had sprung upward and kicked out its hind legs in a buck. Even before the hind legs had again touched ground, the front legs were pawing high into the air. Newberry grabbed at the saddle, to keep from being tumbled backward. It did little good because Thor was already into the fury of his second buck.

Newberry started screaming at Preacher like a madman. Preacher kept silent. There was nothing he could say or do. It was Thor's show.

Randolph was driven from side to side on the saddle of the whipping, slashing, snorting horse.

"The beast has gone mad!" he screamed. "Shoot it! Shoot it!"

Not a single man moved a muscle. The love and respect that Major Newberry thought he had from his men was proving paperthin. When Thor began to spin like a whirling dervish they began to cheer for the horse and not the rider.

Newberry turned ashen as the ferocity of Thor's onslaught increased. He was beginning to realize that the horse had been trained never to be stolen. His dread turned to real fear, knowing that even when he jumped free the horse would paw him to death for not being his master.

But his lungs and heart could take no more of this brutal pounding. He released the reins and pulled his legs away from the horse. It did not slow the horse. In fact, it gave Thor the knowledge that he was winning and he jumped skyward on all fours, thudded back to earth and stopped short. Newberry sailed over the mane and head, without being prepared. He came down hard on his right shoulder, his arm twisting and cracking beneath his own weight.

Thor did not move, but looked at Preacher for his next command. Preacher put out his hand and Thor came at a thankful trot.

Only then was Preacher aware that the spectacle had drawn a circle of some three hundred men who stood silent and awed.

Then there was a moan, a whimper, and near childish

crying. Newberry's right arm had been fractured and he was spewing blood like a chicken whose neck had just been wrung off.

Embarrassed, his men began to tear their shirts into strips to bind up the wound, but the blood soaked the clumsy bandage in seconds. Someone called for a medic, but no one stepped forward.

Preacher cursed. "Damn idiots! Don't want him bleeding to death on me. Reggie, get your sentry's powderhorn."

With a single forward motion he made the shattered bone reenter the wound. Before Newberry was aware, he sprinkled the spewing wound with black powder and set it aflame.

The air was filled with the dreadful odor of searing flesh and then a cry of pain.

"Hansen, get a litter bearer team ready to take Major Newberry to his tent," he said.

"Wait!" Newberry rasped. "Cousin Reggie, I cannot keep that bastard in my unit. His papers are lying there on the field. Do me the honor of filling in my transfer order."

"To who, Cousin Randolph? He's near been through the whole Virginia Command."

Despite his pain Newberry could still grin with malicious candor. "Transfer him to Fort Donelson."

"But, that is in Tennessee."

Newberry rose on his good arm as if preparing to fully rise and do battle. "Exactly! General Gideon Pillow deserves a soldier with a record such as his." Then he glowered at Preacher. "If we both survive this war, which I full intend on doing, we have a challenge date."

"He may have just saved your life," Reggie shouted in disgust.

"Which is the reason I saved it," Preacher mumbled. "I, too, am planning on living through this war. Challenge accepted."

The arrogance returned. "Men, to my tent. He has sullied my reputation, but I shall wait for another day to defend my honor."

Preacher's disgust was like wormwood. Not a single word about the sullied reputation of Rosamond or the wanton woman she had become because of his craving desires.

The thought was also uppermost in Reggie's mind. He was confused, perplexed and felt a little strange with the young man.

This was hardly the James David Preacher he had known as a little tag-along kid. This was a man—hard, cold, and knowledgable. He had been away from home for nearly ten months and the few letters from his mother had been troubling. Preacher troubled him more.

"My apology for so rapidly giving you over to Randolph. Your accusation shocked me, because I have sensed such since he and I have been camped side by side. Still, it is not a subject one discusses about your own sister. Are you sure?"

"Randolph is the one!"

"You will have a chance to stop at home on your way to Ford Donelson," he said slowly, dreading the favor he must ask. "Will you let my mother and father know that I am aware of the truth about Cousin Randolph."

Preacher would not lie. "I can see that they get your message, but not by me personally. Ride out with me, Reggie. I don't want others hearing of our family troubles or how things are back home."

He rode with James David for an hour and then could ride no further. The stories had turned his stomach to bile. That his father could seek this young man's death, again and again, was frightening. That James David had gained such gunman's skill made his three month Army record a travesty of petty jealousy. Now, he wished he could keep him with him, but that could not be. He took the file from his saddlebag, opened it and let the biting January winds briskly take the light sheets of paper away.

"What in the hell are you doing?"

"Wiping out three futile months in the life of J.D. Preacher. Tell your new commander, John Floyd, that I sent you on verbal orders, because your records had not caught up to me."

"Newberry said I was going to General Gideon Pillow."

He laughed sarcastically. "That is true to a degree. They are both there in lock step, ready to trip the other up. I don't envy you being under either bastard. Pillow was President Polk's spy in Mexico and prone not to fight. Floyd gave himself the rank of general when he was Secretary of War under President Buchanan, but no one calls him by any rank.''

"How do you know so much?" Preacher asked on a note of puzzlement.

Reggie spat, as though getting rid of a hated matter. "Since the day I could read I devoured every military history I could lay my hands on. My dream was a military college, but I was duped out of going because my father thought me slow of brain. All that was left for me, like your brother Zach, was to become a Southern loafer. I feel needed for the first time in my life. I wish I was riding on with you. The Union will strike Fort Donelson with fierce revenge.''

"Revenge?"

"Yes, because of Floyd. When he was Secretary of War, he deliberately weakened the Federal striking force and made sure that he approved only southern cadets to West Point. He thought to end the war before it started. Funny thing, though. He will now be up against a man he forced out of the Army, rather than the man facing a court martial for drunkenness. Fiery little cuss by the name of Ulysses S. Grant.''

Preacher frowned. "I know that name. He's bought horses from my mother.''

"What intelligent man has not." He got down from his horse. "I do not offer my hand, J. D. Preacher, because I would not wish my gesture denied. I will work to regain your respect of me as a person, for I dare not discuss your feelings of my family. I would appreciate your not even mentioning my name, if you do stop at home. Keep alive!''

Preacher turned Thor away from the man. He departed with an odd mixture of pity and respect. He would honor the man by not looking back to see him standing alone and dejected.

CHAPTER 7

PREACHER'S FIRST WARNING came at Johnson City. Thor was about ready to throw a shoe and he wanted him reshod. Two blacksmiths closed their barndoors in his face, the third bellowed for all to hear his refusal to serve, but quietly whispered: "My farm is a mile west, Mr. Preacher. Come after dark, Collin Young has spies everywhere."

Preacher would have gone on, but he could not take a chance with Thor. He walked the horse out of Johnson City, and then melted into the woods. He headed west, keeping his eyes on the road, until he saw the blacksmith come along. The man turned into a small, neat farm—and a surprise. Three men in butternut uniforms awaited him. They stayed until after dark. Then, when he was about to give up hope, he saw a figure dart from the farmhouse and into the woods.

The quick, desperate charge of the blacksmith was born of frustration and despair at what was happening to his world.

"I saw where your hoof prints left the road," he panted. "I knew you would be near by. I can only tap the shoe back in place. Ride a mile and walk a mile."

"Can you put this on my mother's account?"

The man snorted. "The militia has closed your family account and several others. I cannot even accept your cash or barter. I would be shot if I even came out to your plantation."

"But, how are people to survive?"

The man spoke in haste and out of bitterness. "Ask your brother. He makes a handsome bank deposit each week for himself and Collin Young."

"Young?"

"The struttin' peacock, with weird rules. Blacks can't leave their plantations, so whites gotta buy and fetch their own wares from town. No horses, livestock or provisions are sold unless approved by Young. Any stranger coming or going must be reported. Go boy, 'fore my wife and brother gets curious about me. He's Young's spy in Johnson City."

The storm started with a few light flakes of snow. Within an hour it was a howling, blinding blizzard. The blacksmith's advise was not needed, Preacher and Thor were both forced to walk. Even though the fury reduced their advance to a crawl, Preacher was aware that a single rider was on his trail.

Entering the north pasture of Bradburn Hill, he kept to the wooded hillside, broke off a dead branch and obscured his tracks even more than the blizzard was doing. His intent was to get to the hickory forest shed and enclosure where stray cows were kept before herding them home. Ruefully, he thought of the enclosure. It was there that he had been forced into his first shootout and killed Calvin Fuller. Just as he was ready to enter the trail, dark forms came out of it.

The stray cows were frightened of the storm and wanted to just lay down and die. Zach and Amos were beating them to keep them on the move. Zachary Preacher resented having to work like a slave, but every head of cattle was becoming worth its weight in gold. Amos saw Preacher first and his face turned frightful.

"Brother?" Zachary gasped.

Then, in a break in the storm, Zach saw another rider crossing the pasture. He stiffened, the cold feeling of dread running along his spine. He had worked hard to get back into the good graces of Collin Young. Now Preacher was back, was being tailed and would ruin everything again. The storm put the man behind a curtain of swirling white.

"Amos!" Zach shouted. "I'll see to the cows. Get my brother to the root cellar and barn his horse. No one must know that he is here!"

Preacher bristled, but held his silence. The trailing man and his brother were bound to meet up in the pasture. Was Zach preparing to sell him out? He was too tired and cold to let it bother him. He knew that the walk trail over the ridge was the fastest way home. Home did not mean the root cellar.

"Mas'sa James David," Amos said, his head bobbing and his tongue slurring, "scares me that he knows of the root cellar."

He lit a candle. A hickory knot brazier had the underground room toasty warm. Bedding was on many of the lower shelves, turning them into bunks.

"Your Ma's been using this as a hiding place for slaves to sneak north. If'n he knows, it means trouble."

"Not if mother is involved."

Amos said nothing as he departed to report to Preacher's mother and Morgana. He had not spun away fast enough before Preacher could see the hatred in his eyes for Zach. The eyes had been unmasked and naked. The hatred in them was absolutely astonishing.

His mother came first, tired and drawn. She brought fresh provisions for his saddlebag, a quick report and a desire for him to leave quickly.

Preacher was aghast to learn that so much had been going wrong in the county and of the power Collin Young had regained. His father seemed to lose, rather than regain his health, and Zachary was nearly the sole master of the plantation.

Even Morgana seemed different, a lack of warmth in her greeting. From a shelf in the root cellar, she pulled down a wooden box which had arrived for him from New Orleans. They were silent as he pried open the lid and took out the top note:

"My darling J.D.—

Normally one sends gifts to the bride. This time the bride sends gifts to her beloved friends.

"By the time you receive this, I shall be Mrs. Giscard d'Chirac and living on his lovely estate, LaFitte Landing. I fear for my dear New Orleans but took your sage advise. My lovely *Maison Blanc* is now owned by my black servants and thus safe, should the Federals invade.

"Your gift, dear J.D. should have been Teton Jack, but my new husband is also an arms dealer and received twelve of these gems from his Whitworth agent in England. Its masculinity was you, including the reloading kit. Until we meet again.

"P.S. Saw Morgan Lake and heard about your brother and his daughter. Your gift is wrapped in one for Morgana."

"Oh, Mother Preacher," Morgana gasped, "his rifle is wrapped in yards and yards of pure white silk. I shall have a wedding dress, after all."

"Wedding?" Preacher asked.

"Yes," Matilda said, but not with great warmth. "Zachary and Morgana are to be wed."

"And I want your blessing," Morgana cried gaily.

Preacher gave her a hug and a kiss, but not verbal blessing.

Amos came in hesitant and reluctant. "Thor is re-shod and Mas'sa Zachary is feedin' dat man in de kitchen."

Preacher did not need to be told what man or why Zach might be feeding him. The nervousness of his mother told him that he might be causing a problem if he stayed any longer. It was a bitter pill to swallow. On a ruse, he sent his mother and Morgana away to fetch him hot food.

"Amos, my old friend, let's go to the barn for Thor. I want to be gone before their return."

"Young mas'sa," Amos complained, "ya'all will die out in this storm."

"Won't be out in it long, Amos. I just thought of a place where no one will think of finding me."

In the barn, Preacher found Thor had also been combed, curried and fed. On a note of near embarrassment, Amos handed Preacher a leather pouch and clay pipe.

"Amos, you know my mother's feeling about the use of the tobacco weed."

"It's what's inside the pouch dat counts, mas'sa. Dat little surprise came from a horse trader who thought your Ma needed it. She told Ole Amos to hide it until the proper day fur its use. Ah feel dat day am here."

That, at least, sent Preacher away with a warmth in his heart. Amos watched him disappear into the storm, his face even grimmer than usual. It was crazy for a man to be going out in this weather. Plain damn foolishness. He kicked angrily at the snow and, blowing on his hands, went back into the barn. He did not see that Zachary Preacher had been watching from the kitchen window. Within a few minutes, the lone rider from Johnson City was on Preacher's trail again.

For the first few miles, it wasn't bad. Preacher had left in a lull in the storm, but now the wind was increasing and the temperature was going down rapidly. He made no attempt to hide his tracks. Ahead of him was a flat unbroken sheet of whiteness. Still, there was no need for immediate worry. Thor could find the road as long as it was possible to see the trees on either side, and if the storm got no worse, he would make his destination without trouble. It was beginning to grow dark and, for the first time, Preacher began to feel the heavy, insidious cold sliding under his thick coat. He knew he should be close to the turnoff and reined Thor back to a maddening slowness.

Then he cursed. Ahead of them, through the swirling, menacing vortex of flying snow, was a glow of lights. Langhorne Oaks. He jerked on the reins to turn Thor and the horse started around, but they were now facing into the storm. The sharp cold pulled the nostrils of man and horse together with each indrawn breath. Their previous tracks were not yet drifted over, so that Thor picked his way back without too much difficulty. Although the snow had greatly altered the scene, Preacher found the turn off and a moment later the secret cabin in the woods.

He carried his saddlebags into the cabin, dumped them on the cot, lit the kerosene lamp and put the tobacco pouch and pipe on the table. He piled wood into the small fireplace till the roaring crackling fire flung the heat out in waves. Then, he sat down and waited. His wait was not long.

Light and wood smoke pulled the man and snorting horse like a magnet. Warmth and safety from the storm were now more important than mission. He tied his horse next to Thor and did not hesitate in knocking.

"Latch is off," Preacher called.

"Obliged," the man chattered, going immediately to the fireplace. "Got lost in the storm."

Preacher said nothing. He took the clay pipe and planted it between his even white teeth. This done, he opened the rectangular leather pouch and extracted a tobacco length. With casual calm he began to break off shreds of tobacco from the pig-tailed knot of burleigh and place it in a little heap on the table.

Because the brim of his hat kept his eyes in shadow, it appeared that his full concentration was on preparing his smoke. Instead, he was sizing up the man.

The man was a young giant and the fit of the Confederate grey suggested that in no way could the uniform have been stolen. He was too spit and polish and bore the chevrons of a Lance Corporal. In spite of his military bearing, Preacher still sensed something amiss. The brown eyes, swimming in vast pools of clear, milky white, were defiant and cagey, completely devoid of friendliness.

Preacher looked up from his preoccupation with the tobacco and grinned. "Get separated from your troop, soldier?"

"Nope." Now that warmth was returning, so could his mission.

"Too bad," Preacher said, picking at his burleigh and increasing his heap. "On my way to Fort Donelson and thought a nearby troop could re-supply me."

"You don't look like no soldier, what with no uniform and a fancy horse in need of a shoe." His moon face went suddenly grave. He had all but admitted that he had been tracking the man. "That loose shoe helped me find my way to your kind fire."

Preacher ignored the obvious lie, assuming the man did not know that Thor was reshod at Bradburn Hill. He started to reach for another length of burleigh pig-tail and paused, his fingers just within the open flap of the pouch. "Yeah, a bad night for a horse to start to throw a shoe. Stopped in Johnson City and not a single blacksmith would help me. Thought a man by the name of Ernest Roby was going to help me, but he didn't."

There was an infinitesimal hesitation, then the soldier's face twisted. "If you must know, that man is my brother-in-law and suspected by Captain Collin Young, our military police authority, of being a Union sympathizer. He was caught earlier this evening giving aid and comfort to the enemy. The thrashing he got will be long remembered."

The concentration of bitterness and defiance in the voice made Preacher see plainly what had happened to the poor blacksmith.

"That's an odd statement to make to a stranger," Preacher said curtly. "How do you know I am not that enemy he was helping?"

"Because your horse's shoe was not repaired in Johnson City, Mister Jeremy James David Preacher. I was sent to find out why a known killer was back in our territory."

"Then they should have sent someone more experienced. I knew you were behind me, even before the storm broke."

The taunt stung like a whiplash. The muscles tightened into hard knots under the fabric of the tunic. His face got mottled.

"Experienced? I didn't need to track you to find my way to your plantation. I used to come as an assistant to my brother-in-law. God, you were a mean and nasty kid."

"I don't know of what you speak."

"Every man should know the truth from the man who is about to kill him." The voice was goading, rhythmic, excited. "Hear tell they call you the Widow Maker because of your fast draw. You ain't got no weapon and I ain't got no wife. But I got a memory. It was your fifth birthday and your ma had given you a pony. The yard was full of rich plantation kids getting a pony ride and eating cake and custard. I had to stand and watch while Ernest worked with your slave in the blacksmith shop. When no one had any more interest in the pony, I went to take a ride. Even though I was ten, you ran and grabbed me out of the saddle, wrestled me to the ground and rammed my face down into a pile of the pony's shit."

"Oh, yes!" Preacher grinned. "And as I recall, my dear brother Zachary came to your aid. He reported it to our father and I got a thrashing for not sharing my gift." Preacher

reached into the pouch for more tobacco. "And it is Zachary
to your aid again. Did you enjoy your hot meal before trailing
me again?"

"Shut up, bastard!"

The man drew a revolver from his holster with less than
expert ease.

Preacher watched the working of the man's face, saw the
big finger shake on the firing trigger of the weapon. Preacher
could sense and smell that the man, whose name he could not
recall, had never killed before.

"Don't do it, soldier," he said, softly. "It's hardly a thing
to kill me over."

"You son of a bitch," he said hoarsely, "that has nothing
to do with it. Captain Young has a handsome reward out for
you, dead or alive. Your brother just sweetened the pot if it
were dead only."

Their eyes locked. Beads of nervous sweat broke out on the
soldier's forehead, and suddenly, though there was no
outward evidence of it, Preacher knew the man had prepared
himself to do murder. Survival meant staring the man down,
so he did not see the movement of Preacher's right hand
within the tobacco pouch. His thumb found and pulled back
the hammer on the twelve ounce, four inch derringer. He had
but a single shot, but at such close range the .44 caliber pellet
would keep the man's weapon silent.

The explosion was slight, producing a perfectly round hole
in the leather pouch and a slightly larger hole in the broad,
white forehead. Even as Preacher had fired, instinct had him
rolling out of the chair and across the dirt floor. When he
looked back the man was still staring at the spot where
Preacher had sat, but no longer realizing his eyes would stare
permanently. Then, his knees gave way and he sat back into
the fireplace. Flames began to lick up each side of his thighs.

Preacher started to pull him from the fire, then hesitated.
Such an *accident* might suit him better. By the time he was
found, it would be assumed that he had sought shelter from
the storm and the cabin burned during the night. He turned
the lamp over on the table, so it, too, would ignite, took his
saddlebags and went outside to Thor.

His next instinct was to return to Bradburn Hill and confront his brother with the man's charge.

"That will have to wait," he told himself dully, heading back into the storm.

CHAPTER 8

WINTER STAYED WITH him until he reached Nashville. There was no way he could face another hundred miles of winter saddle travel. He bought the cheapest "man and beast" passage on a Cumberland river packet.

Preacher sat on the edge of a steel cot in the riverboat's hold and stared ahead of him into nothingness. The hold was icy cold and no blanket had been provided. Now that he was no longer constantly in the saddle, he felt little of anything except a paralyzing numbness. It made him incapable of thought, oblivious to emotion. Several times, other men traveling in the hold called for him to join them to eat. He didn't answer them and stirred only to feed and water Thor.

On the morning of the second day, when the other men were up having breakfast, he heard the paddlewheel engine slow to a stop and then he was jolted from the cot as the boat slammed hard into something solid. The passageway was filled with screaming people and it was a struggle to fight his way to the deck and up to the bridge. The captain was screaming at the deck hands to get a gangway laid out to the river bank, into which he had purposely rammed his vessel. The purser, yelling just as loud, was advising the passengers to disembark there or face a return trip to Nashville. A man with a red flag was being rowed away from the boat and back to the center of the river.

"Captain, I'm a soldier going to Fort Donelson. Why this stop?"

"Armored gunboats have made them surrender Fort Henry on the Tennessee River."

Preacher shook his head. "But, sir, I don't understand. We are on the Cumberland River, as is Fort Donelson."

The gray-whiskered old riverman looked at him with piteous contempt. "Boy, you don't know the area. There's only ten land miles between Fort Henry, Fort Donelson and the two rivers. We got warned in time that the gunboats are going back up to the Ohio River and will churn right back down the Cumberland."

"But, won't that take time?"

The man spat. "Ain't the gunboats turning me back, lad. Some Union General by the name of Grant landed 15,000 troops at Fort Henry and is marching them overland. His cannon could sink me as sure as a gunboat. Best get your mount and make tracks. They'll need every soldier they can muster."

"A general named Grant," Preacher mused to himself, as he got Thor and his equipment ashore. "The man was only a Colonel when I left Virginia. The war seems to be moving at a faster clip in these parts."

That fact became more apparent as he worked his way along the south bank of the Cumberland. The river began to fill with small vessels rapidly going south east. Then, suddenly, there was no more flat river bank to follow. A rocky bluff rose some five-hundred feet right out of the water, forcing him inland and onto a rough trail up the back side of the bluff. To his surprise, the top of the bluff was a rolling plateau dotted with wooded groves. He urged Thor to a high spot and sat gasping.

Below him was the vista of the river valley and the panorama of battle. Beyond the river, the woods and marsh-lands were so filled with blue uniforms that it looked like the river had flooded its banks. However, he saw that some com-mander had made a tactical error. Row boats were being brought to the river bank, but the soldiers would never be able to scale the steep bluffs to the fort.

Low booming, like a coming thunderstorm, turned his attention up river. The paddlewheel captain had been wise to turn back when he had. Six ironclad gunboats were coming full steam down the river and firing on the Confederate gun placements. It would take them awhile to reach the fort, which sat on the edge of the bluff and was using its well-mounted and well-manned guns to lob artillery fire into the opposite bank. Above the fort, the woods were as gray with Confederate uniforms as the lower woods were blue.

He rode forward, keeping his eyes alert so he could report on all that he saw. What he thought was a single bluff and plateau proved to be several and it took him some time to get on the same plateau as the fort. By then the gunboats were attacking the fort and were under equal attack. The Union gunners were unable to get enough elevation and their shells were exploding harmlessly into the bluff cliff. The Fort Donelson men only had to shoot downward with deadly aim. Puff after puff exploded so rapidly that the fort was covered in its own smoke screen.

A cannon carrier came rumbling along with six riflemen in pursuit. They set up on the bluff's edge and the riflemen began to fire.

"Hey, you!" the cannon officer called. "Get your weapon and help out!"

Preacher knew that rifle fire would be wasted at that distance, but his youthful excitement in being asked overcame that fact. He pulled a Whitworth he had received from an old friend from its scabbard and ran to join the group. The slim, beautifully fashioned weapon was so light he felt strange in handling it.

Just then two of the gunboats exploded as one, filling the sky with a fireworks show. They sank almost at once. Bugles blared over the explosions of the Donelson shells. The gunboats were pulling back to care for their wounded. All except one gunboat. It was adrift in the downstream current. Preacher expected to hear the cannon officer prepare for this coming target and turned to look at him.

Only then did he realize that the cannon was fake. The officer had also shouldered a rifle. The pitiful shots were landing in the water well short of the gunboat.

Preacher dropped to his right knee, raised the Whitworth and squinted. The sun glinted on the insignia of an officer's cap. It was a good target, even though he knew the shell would never reach that far. He fired.

His first surprise was in the recoil. He had felt only a slight thump to his shoulder. His second surprise was in the disappearance of the officer's cap.

The gunboat was some 2,000 yards below and upriver. Before the sound ever reached the naval officer's ears, the Whitworth's hexagonal slug struck the tall crowned cap and sent it flying. Preacher had to be sure it was his weapon and not the wind. Sailors were hurriedly bringing heavy planks onto the deck. He aimed for a plank in a sailor's arms. He fired and almost at once the plank was spun from the sailor's hands and into the river. Joy turned into realization.

The front of a cannon had been hoisted up and the planks placed to give it elevation. The gunboat was not adrift, it was stalling for the work to be completed. The Donelson guns were silent so the wounded could be taken from the other gunboats. Preacher pulled back the hammer, putting another 530 grain bullet into the chamber. He took careful aim at the gunner aligning the cannon. It took just the slightest touch to squeeze off the trigger. To his ears, there was only a slight pop but the sailor died before the shot's sound could reach him. His mate, ready to ignite the fuse, shook the gunner's shoulders as though he had just fainted.

Preacher fired again. The mate grabbed at his chest and dropped the flaming torch into the black powder keg. The cannon and two dead sailors disappeared in a cloud of blue-black explosive smoke. The boat began to list and sink.

The cannon officer and his riflemen stood silent and puzzled, looking at the Whitworth.

Preacher saw the error at once. The rifle was a frightening gift, but the gleam in the officer's eyes told him it could also be a danger. As a gunslinger, he had learned to watch a man's eyes and then his hands. With this weapon he couldn't even tell if the man's eyes were open or not.

"Who are you and what is that weapon?"

"My name and the weapon don't matter. I am here from the Virginia Command to report to General Gideon Pillow."

The man stood without moving, without saying anything, his eyes burning at the rifle. He bit his lip and tried to keep his voice level. "I want you and that piece in my cannon command. I'm Lieutenant Fletcher Brooks."

"I don't want your name," Preacher said brutally. "You

saw nothing! Take credit for lucky fire down on the gunboat and leave it at that!''

He whistled up Thor, carefully put the rifle back in its scabbard and purposely rode to the northeast. An inlet made his detour even longer and when he turned back west, he found himself coming up on the back of a mounted Confederate troop camp.

"Stand down and be recognized!"

Preacher found himself looking down the barrels of two sentry rifles. Before he could respond, he was greeted by a turkey call yell from an officer bounding through the woods.

"Brent! Brent Barrett!" he cried out.

"Let him through," Brent called gaily to the sentries. "Follow me to our section, boy. I can't stop to welcome you right now."

Preacher rode to catch up with his friend. He did not know what Brent meant by their section, but he saw other cavalry soldiers turn and look at Brent with envious pride. All that mattered to Preacher was that if Brent was there, it meant Morgan Lake would be there as well. He shivered over the thrill of getting to see his mentor again.

Brent jumped from his horse and joined a ring of officers. Preacher followed suit, but with hesitation until he spotted Morgan in the group. The old mentor gave Preacher a sly wink and touched a finger to his lips for silence. Preacher nearly burst with pride. Morgan wore the uniform of a Colonel and Brent that of a Major. Nor did Preacher have to question the name of the man Brent reported to with a smart salute.

Brigadier General Nathan Bedford Forrest reminded Preacher of the picture of Moses in his mother's Bible, except the man's flowing beard was black as night, as were his dark, expressive eyes. His voice boomed like rolling thunder.

"Not new gunboats?"

"No, General. The upriver batteries were able to see their names clearly. They are Commodore Andrew Foote's boats that attacked Fort Henry."

"How did they get here?"

"Up the Tennessee to the Ohio and back down the

Cumberland.'' Preacher gulped, realizing he had spoken without thinking.

"Excuse me, General,'' Morgan jumped in. "This is the young gunman I've boasted on in the past—James David Preacher.''

Forrest nodded. "Lad seems to know the territory.''

"Sorry, sir, but I don't. That's only information I gained from the riverboat captain 'fore he put us ashore and turned back.''

The General frowned until his beetle brows were attacking each other. "Why would they stop their attack on Fort Henry and switch to Fort Donelson?'' Because he was looking skyward, no one answered. Then he glared at Preacher. "If you were at the river, how many troops did the gunboats unload?''

He said, unsteadily, "None, sir. A General Grant is reported to have brought 15,000 toops overland. It's only ten miles from Fort Henry to the Cumberland.''

Brent grew uneasy. "That would fit with the rumor I was bringing back from the fort. General Pillow, it seems, felt Fort Henry was indefensible. No one is sure, but they say they were ordered to retreat south and surrender the fort.''

"Damn!'' Forrest boomed. "The only retreat they were to have made was overland and canoe to us.''

Preacher shook his head. "Those canoes are in Union hands, General. However, they have them so far down river that they are below the bluff cliffs. They can only cross if they go downstream. From the bluff, a good sentry can see their every move.''

The General pursed his lips. He was not over five-feet-nine. The top of his head barely came level with Preacher's chin and he couldn't have weighed more than one-hundred and twenty pounds, but he was the kind of a man who could lead an assault on hell with a Roman candle. When he liked people, his sharp hazel eyes had a warm twinkle to them. When he didn't like people, or found them difficult, his eyes were apt to be like twin rapiers. They were like rapiers now. He wasted no time on formalities.

"A sentry I am not allowed, being under the temporary

command of two jackals. Barrett, send a man back to keep his ears open at the fort. Whatever Floyd and Pillow are up to, I want to know at once. And, young man, I thank you for your quick eyes and listening ears. Nor did I need to be told you were a Preacher. That is a Matilda Preacher horse if I have ever seen one. I trust that your beautiful mother is well?''

Preacher had never thought of his mother as beautiful, but respected the comment coming from such a gentlemen. "As well as the war allows, sir.''

Then the warm twinkle vanished and turned back to rapiers. "It is a most handsome horse and your pistol's braced nicely, with a scabbard and rifle. However, my boy, spare me having to turn you down as a recruit. They provision me for only a hundred men and I am five over at present.''

"Thank you for the thought, sir," Preacher said with respect. "But I am here on verbal orders from the Virginia Command to report to the Fort Commander, John Floyd, and to General Gideon Pillow.''

"Lucky for them, unlucky for you," he said honestly. Then he laughed. "Perhaps you are the eyes and ears I need around these two military ninnies. Tarry with your friends, Preacher, for it is time for our midday meal.''

The meal sounded great, for Preacher couldn't recall when last he had eaten and Morgan and Brent were anxious for news about Morgana and the Barrett plantation.

Even as they ate and talked, Preacher's eyes kept roaming. It was a unit set apart, with its own field kitchen, horse grooms, distinctive uniforms and fine weapons. Preacher could tell by the mold of each man's legs that they had been born to the saddle. It wasn't ego telling him that he was still better than a majority of them.

Morgan Lake saw his glances and knew Preacher well. As a Missouri militia leader, he had taken Preacher's natural talents with a gun and molded him into a fast draw expert. He wanted Preacher with him again and resented the foolish figure of one hundred men that General Pillow insisted upon. The name of his daughter brought him back into the conversation.

"It just makes me sick to think of that lovely Morgana marrying your damn brother!''

Preacher and Morgan looked at Brent thoughtfully and then at each other. They had to hide their smiles. It was the first indication they had that Brent Barrett had an interest in Morgana. The only time he had met the young woman was when he had brought a Confederate troop to Missouri. He had all but ignored her at the time.

"Barrett," a cavalryman called, coming into camp, "some damn cannon officer is spreading the rumor that there's a Virginia Command guy here with a new weapon. Claims it knocked out one of those gunboats at 2,000 yards."

"Don't they respect your rank?" Preacher asked, trying to change the subject.

"All the respect in the world, James David. We are a raider outfit and will always have a high mortality rate. We go by last names so we don't get too close and personal. We get there first with the most men, as the old man says."

Morgan laughed. "Of course our men have changed that to 'git there fustest with the mostest.' Sorry you can't be with us—"

Preacher stopped him short. "Just make it Preacher, please. Thor needs a walk." He lowered his voice to a whisper. "Walk along. I got some tall explaining to do."

"I will gladly walk Thor," Morgan grinned, making sure everyone heard. "Thor was the Norse god of thunder and helper in war. He was a youth god armed with a magic hammer that was like silent lightning and always returned to him after being cast."

Preacher gulped. Morgan had all but described his new weapon, but that had to wait until they were quite alone. He let them gain distance from the camp as he related his experience with the Virginia Command and why Reggie Langhorne sent him to Fort Donelson on verbal orders.

"How many damn enemies do we have to fight?" Brent stormed.

"We also have a few friends," Preacher grinned. He took the slim, beautifully fashioned weapon and handed it to Morgan Lake. He pointed at a farmer's land marker.

Lake sighted down the long barrel and crisply pulled the piece's trigger. The hammer fell on a percussion cap and flame blossomed from the rifle's muzzle as its bullet sang down the field for 600 yards to pierce the iron plate of the lot line.

Brent Barrett silently tried his luck, with the same results. Morgan and Lake looked at each other and Brent went for the general.

"It came from Jean-Luc. Her new husband is an arms dealer. It also came wrapped in silk for Morgana's wedding dress."

Morgan pursed his lips. "He's more than an arms dealer, Preacher. He's French, rich and powerful." He paused. "What do you think of the wedding?"

"It's what she wants," Preacher mumbled. But there was a thing in his tone that Morgan didn't like. Something more than resentment, a nuance, a timbre of hatred. He let the subject drop.

"Have I told you how nice it is to see you and have you here."

"I wish I could stay. I could sure use some training on this new piece. You made me mainly a pistol man."

Morgan roared in total delight. He rose, his seven feet still towering over Preacher's six-foot-two. It pleased him that his favorite pupil still regarded him as a teacher, intelligent to still seek answers. He was about to admit that he had a lot to learn about the Whitworth when General Forrest returned with Brent.

The cavalryman stopped short. His eyes glistened as he took the Whitworth from Preacher and handled it like a bride on her wedding night.

"In the spring of 1857," he said dreamily, "my parents and I were house guests of Sir Joseph Whitworth, a distant cousin on my mother's side of the Bedford line. He was a most remarkable mechanical engineer who did the tooling design for the royal arsenal at Enfield Locks. Because of my interest I was shown a working model of an unnamed piece that consistently outshot the Enfield. Sir Joseph said it would never be manufactured because it was too expensive, ammunition difficult to manufacture—" He halted. "The gunboat. It was not a rumor. How into your hands, Preacher?"

Preacher related the story of his gift from Jean-Luc.

"So," Nathan Bedford Forrest drawled. "Giscard d'Chirac would mean Cook and Brothers of New Orleans. The man has a finger in every side of this war. How many did he receive, I wonder?"

"If I recall, the note said her husband had received twelve from his Whitworth agent in London."

"It is too dangerous to wire from the fort," he said grimly and not making sense to the other three. But that was why he was proving to be a great tactical officer. His inner brain was always working out a problem, while his tongue related only the tip of the iceberg. "It is only a rumor, but if Pillow gets his hands on this man and weapon it will become fact. A fact he will not know how to deal with."

He began to pace, tossing the light rifle from hand to hand. Morgan and Brent knew the coals in hell were being bellowed to white hot. When he turned his words were as rapier as his eye flashes.

"Barrett! Pillow is in the field. Find a man and clothing to match this lad. Give him one of our best Pattern 1853 Enfield longarms and send him to the fort. We must make the cannon officer look foolish for such a rumor. Preacher, are you a betting man?"

The afternoon was chilling down rapidly. His words came out as white vapor puffs. "Depending upon the bet," Preacher said, unafraid of the man.

"It's handsome!" Forrest boomed. "Memphis is a good hundred and fifty miles southwest. It is February 7th, in the years of our Lord 1862. Get to my family plantation, wire New Orleans for every available Whitworth, return them to me in seven days and you win the bet."

"Seven days!" Morgan roared. "General, who can tell where we will be in seven—"

"Here and waiting," Nate Forrest went on imperturbably. "Sam Grant sits down the river with a new star and a box of cigars to chew upon. His craw is full of Floyd and Pillow, but he's too sharp to forfeit his new generalship on petty revenge. He knows damn well our supply boats arrived yesterday and he now has control of the upper Tennessee and lower Ohio

Rivers. If he is the same Sam Grant who was brilliant in the Mexican wars, he knows he can put us in a seven to ten day siege. I say seven, because when he rolls soldiers' dice, he always bets the seven.''

''He's not one of our men to order about,'' Brent shrugged, nodding towards Preacher.

The scathing look from Forrest was withering. ''A Field Commander grabs the nearest body he can find for messenger service. For the moment, he is mine—'' Then he grinned, ''and if he wins, he is still mine, even if I have to shoot six good men to make room for him.''

Preacher stood there and was without an answer. In that instant he knew it was not his war and possibly not their war. They were infighting amongst themselves much as the Army of Virginia.

Later, he couldn't even recall Morgan and Brent's last words to him. He and Thor burned up the miles to Memphis. In a way he resented the bet because Forrest wanted more to get his hands on the Whitworth rifles than on James David Preacher. He arrogantly knew that he was as good, if not better, than the majority of them, with or without his Whitworth. Still, he wanted to win, to be a part of Forrest's Raiders.

Ironically, as the miles melted away, he thought of the men who would be the real winners if the South prevailed— Jarvis McPhee, his brother, Michael Langhorne, and men such as they who would use victory to make slavery three times as cruel.

Thor plodded ahead while he drowsed in the saddle. Some dreams were peaceful—the quiet songs of the plantation folk as the day came to an end. Other dreams were lonely— the cold eyes of a gunfighter calling you out to put your name on a gravestone.

Thor stopped short and snorted with alarm. Preacher came awake and blinked to clear his eyes. He was facing two Confederate officers, a man with a shining badge and their drawn guns.

''You all right, boy?''

Before Preacher could answer the man with the badge, an

officer barked. "Ah'm not concerned, Sheriff, if he's all right, but who he is!"

Preacher looked around. Before him was a small town, behind him, swarming the fields like a blight of locusts, were an army in gray uniforms.

Because the man with the star had addressed him gently, Preacher addressed him in kind. "Quite fine, sir. Just fell asleep in the saddle. Long ride from Fort Donelson. Might I inquire my location?"

"Milan, Tennessee, son."

"Boy!" the officer barked. "You will report only to me and not this local officer."

"Are you the retreat forces who deserted Fort Henry?"

The officer looked up belligerently. "What do you mean?"

Preacher's staccato voice snapped back almost before the officer had the words out of his mouth. "The fort was surrendered without proper authority. I am on orders from General Nathan Bedford Forrest, so stand aside. I must get to the telegraph in Memphis."

"We have a couple of Milan boys with the General," Sheriff Wesley Thorpe said proudly. "Why not use our telegraph depot?"

The suggestion pleased Preacher, but he wanted to keep the officer off guard. "Only if the Federals aren't tapping into your line, Sheriff. They've got gunboats on the Tennessee, and Yankee spies all over. There are 15,000 blue uniforms keeping Fort Donelson under siege. Seems the boys from Fort Henry were to march the ten miles to help them, but disappeared."

The officer drew his lips back tautly against his teeth. "I left under orders from General Pillow."

Preacher grinned. "General Forrest says a Field Commander has to grab at opportunities and make his own decisions."

The officer's face turned a shade redder. He ran his tongue over his lips and turned to his aide. "Prepare to march. We will go back to Fort Donelson."

"Come," Sheriff Thorpe grinned, "I'll wake up the depot

operator.''

Preacher weas unsure where he might find J.T., so he sent messages to both the *Maison Blanc* and LaFitte Landing. He prayed an answer would be waiting when he reached the Forrest family plantation.

More than an answer awaited his arrival late the next day. He barely had time to give Mrs. Forrest news of her husband before she shooed him to the plantation's private dock on the Mississippi. There, he found a sparkling, brand new paddlewheeler bearing the name *Jean-Luc*. It also bore the standard of Emperor Napolean III of France. He recalled being told that J.T.'s husband was a Frenchman, but didn't quite understand a French vessel with heavily armed French sailors being on the Mississippi. The moment he got down from Thor, he was approached by a tall man in a starched white suit. The man wore a broad-brimmed Panama hat which shadowed his face. When he was within ten feet of Preacher, he swept. it off in a cavalier bow. Now Preacher could see that the man was quite old, with a pruned face, glowing white hair, but was impressively mustachoed.

''Good morning, *monsieur*,'' he said. ''Giscard d'Chirac at your service.''

''J.T.'s new husband?'' Preacher gasped.

The moustache didn't even twitch. ''The sailors do not speak English, *Monsieur* Preacher, but have orders to bring your mount on board. Is that a problem?''

''Not if I am going aboard, as well.''

The man snorted and went up the gangway. Two sailors took Thor up another gangway and down into the hold. Preacher wanted to follow Thor, but walked behind d'Chirac. Without comment, the man took him into a passageway. Two sailors fell in behind them.

Preacher didn't look back. ''Is your wife on the—''

He never got to finish the sentence. A sailor shoved him roughly into an open cabin door. Preacher crashed to the floor. Suddenly there was a knife at Preacher's throat. Giscard d'Chirac came into the cabin and put a hand on the French sailor's arm. The sailor shook the arm off angrily but the old man seized his shoulder and spoke quickly.

"There will be no bloodshed. Lock him in until we get to Paducah."

He went to the door. He seemed about to go out, but then turned back. He spat contemptuously at Preacher's feet. Without waiting to see the result of his action, he turned on his heel and started out again.

It was a mistake. Preacher covered the distance to the door in two huge strides. He seized the tall man by the back of the neck and the belt and hurled him bodily back into the cabin. The Frenchman fell heavily. He was half stunned.

The two sailors were immediately upon Preacher. One hit him across the face with a back-handed swipe that started the blood spurting from his nose, as the other took an arm and twisted it behind his back. Preacher gave him an elbow to the stomach and the man doubled in pain.

A curt voice said, "You promised me no trouble, *monsieur.*"

Preacher turned. It was like seeing a ghost. Jarvis McPhee, his nemesis from Missouri, stood in the doorway. He slipped his gun out of his holster. "I said I wanted this one kept alive until I am ready for him. d'Chirac, get out of here! You two, get his weapons and lock him in."

The sight of the gun broke the last barrier of Preacher's control. McPhee's gun was uncocked so Preacher lunged forward. The squat man amazingly side-stepped neatly and brought the barrel of the gun down on Preacher's skull. Preacher knew he had played the fool even as he staggered back into the cabin like a wounded bull coming up out of a wallow.

The second sailor, built like an ox, pinned both of his arms back and got his mouth right up to Preacher's ear. "Don't play the young fool, *monsieur,*" he whispered in broken English. "Faint! For the sake of Madame d'Chirac, faint!"

Preacher had never fainted in his life. Still, he reasoned this sailor must be under J.T.'s orders. He swayed for a moment then let his knees buckle. He went down.

McPhee put the gun back in its holster and grinned.

"Very neat, d'Chirac. A lot of people will be happy when you put him ashore at Carauthersville with me. Donelson, take his weapons to our cabin and get out of that silly garb.''

Preacher cursed himself. He had been led up a garden path and he had an unpleasant suspicion that when he got to the end he wasn't going to like the view. McPhee could have killed him on the spot, and he had justification. He had cut McPhee's trail too many times and cost him a slew of his gunfighters, slaves and stolen contraband. The connection between the guerrilla leader and d'Chirac left him puzzled. And what part did J.T. play in all of this?

He heard the sounds of departure, which startled him. Night was falling quickly and night travel on the Mississippi was dangerous in the wintertime.

As soon as the paddlewheeler came to a midstream course, the French sailor returned and silently motioned for Preacher to follow him. He was taken to another cabin and left alone.

Preacher had been in riverboat cabins before, but never a stateroom of such size and opulence. Everything was done in shades of white, from the blond furniture, to silk upholstery, to the canopy of the double sized four-poster bed. The only color in the room were vases of fresh cut flowers, out of keeping with the month of February and bitter winds coming down the Mississippi. He knew that not even New Orleans would have flowers at this time of the year. He heard the sharp French of d'Chirac, answered by a soft French-Creole. But only the woman entered the stateroom.

"My, my, my," Jean Luc purred in beautiful mezzo soprano. "It has been a long time, my young friend. But, no longer young. Let me feast my eyes on this new found maturity.''

Preacher did not respond, for he, too, was feasting his eyes. He had seen Jean Luc Trauffaunt in many guises, from the gaudy gowned madam of the most fashionable whore house in New Orleans to a nude, playful kitten. He knew her to be a woman somewhere in her early thirties, for her real age was one of her best kept secrets. Still, he was not prepared for this elegant woman in a Paris gown, as slender of waist as a girl of sixteen. He felt instant arousal, because the gown revealed that she was still full breasted and the sky blue eyes always held a secret sexual glint.

J.T. laughed gaily and determined not to mention how he

looked from the recent fight. "As always, J.D., I can read you like an open book. Suddenly, I became out-of-bounds married property. Sit! The decanter on the table holds something that is not prohibited to either of us. Teton Jack."

"Shall your husband be joining us?" he growled.

With elegant grace she took a seat and poured them each a crystal glass of the amber liquid. "Do you recall your jealousy over my having dinner with my Chicago lawyer, when you thought he was a client?" she teased.

"Until you told me he was married and his wife sat in the next room as you discussed business."

She leaned forward across the table and her voice became curiously intense. "Then try to follow this. You know of my banking in Chicago and that the *Maison Blanc* is now owned by my former servants and girls. What you do not know is that I also have large bank holdings in Mexico City. Business, my young friend. Giscard was land poor in Louisiana and Mexico, but still of French birth and citizenship. With France taking over Mexico, I needed protection and Giscard needed my money to bring him to the attention of the court of Napolean. Dear boy, you've seen him. He can't even get it up anymore to be a proper husband."

"Which means?" he asked, tasting his Teton Jack with relish.

"A tight rope act. Giscard is an envoy between Napolean and Emperor Maximilian of Mexico. As such, he must stay neutral between the governments of the United States and the Confederate States."

"I get lost in the politics of this war, but not in the company a man keeps."

Jeannie swore in Creole. She got up and paced the room. "I warned Giscard he could not take the envoy position and still be an arms dealer. When your request arrived I went to Cook and Brothers, thinking Giscard was no longer associated with them. Of the twenty weapons they had received from England—not twelve, as I was told—they had fifteen left. I purchased them for you and brought them to the Jean-Luc which had just arrived back from Mexico. Jarvis McPhee was also boarding. I recognized his name and your marvelous description of him. He is the most bantam legged man I have ever seen. But, to my point. Giscard, the blithering idiot, has the hold of this vessel filled with guns and ammuntion he is smuggling in for McPhee.''

"Why smuggled in?"

"This is a ship flying the flag of a neutral country," she said hard and crisp. "Giscard is on his way to Paducah to meet with General Henry Halleck of the Department of Ohio, to assure President Lincoln that neither France, nor Mexico, will enter the war. Who knows what McPhee wants with the cargo. If we were searched by either Yankees or Rebels, it would look like an act of war on the part of France and Mexico."

Preacher laughed. "But, didn't you say you had purchased fifteen Whitworth rifles for me?"

Jeannie cracked the faintest suspicion of a smile. "It is not quite the same, and they are not in the hold in weapons crates. I had to have a very sound reason for Giscard to stop at the Forrest plantation landing 'for you, and once I saw McPhee aboard, I knew I had to come along."

She rose and went to a curtain closing off another room in the suite. She pulled back the curtain to reveal a casket on a bier. "It took a few tears to convince Giscard that I had an obligation to transport the dead aunt of a dear friend to Paducah and that we had to stop and take you along. Your rifles are in the casket."

"Is that the reason for all the flowers?"

She downed a shot of Teton Jack in a single swallow. "Giscard always brings me back mounds of fresh flowers from Mexico because he knows he has made my life very bland. I miss the nightly excitement of the customers, the music, the squabbles of the girls. This is the most excitement I have had in months."

"Not very interesting if we are both prisoners of Jarvis McPhee."

"Are we?" She dug into the cleavage of her gown and brought forth a ring of keys. "The master keys for every lock on this vessel. You help me, I'll help you. I want to know what weapons Giscard plans on selling McPhee. They must not fall into his hands, J.D." She turned serious. "New Orleans is doomed. With the Union about to control the

Cumberland, Tennessee, Ohio and Mississippi rivers, my lovely city will be open for an attack from Admiral Farragut's fleet sitting in the Gulf of Mexico.''

"How do you know so much?''

"Intelligence,'' she smirked. "I would have made one hell of a General.'' She sobered. "Most of my information and help has come from Sam Cook. He's not happy being an arms dealer for the war. He used to work the river country before he settled in New Orleans. He knows the ilk of Jarvis McPhee and did not want those fifteen Whitworths falling into guerrilla hands. I fear there may be ten times that number in the hold.

"There is the dinner bell. We are to arrive in Carauthersville just after 1:00 A.M. That gives you just a little over eight hours. If you need help you may count on Jacques, but trust no other. Go now, for Giscard will be here shortly to take me to the dining salon.''

Preacher locked himself in his cabin, washed his face and listened to the tramp of boots in the passageway and up to the main deck. It was easy to tell the tread of McPhee and Donelson from the sailors, for the French sailors wore hobnailed boots to better grip the deck.

His first chore was to retrieve his weapons. Soon he found the stables.

A groom was attending to four stabled horses, one of them Thor. The manner of his dress told Preacher that the boy was Mexican. Sailors had brought Thor onboard, so Preacher decided to gamble that the boy would not know who he was, but would expect a master to come and check on his mount.

The boy shrugged at his greeting. *"No habla English, senor.''*

Preacher thought it was just as well. He patted Thor and saw that he was well groomed and fed. But his eyes were really on the saddle rack. The rifle was still in its scabbard and his saddlebags had not been opened. He took a coin from his pocket, patted the boy on the shoulder and pressed the coin into his hand. He won a friend who did not notice that he did not leave by the same route as he had entered.

Actually, he had little trouble finding the weapon and ammunition crates. That part of the hold was devoid of everything but the six long rifle boxes and four squat ammunition boxes. And it was apparent that McPhee had inspected the goods between New Orleans and Memphis, for one crate had been pried open.

Preacher whistled to himself. The crate contained twelve new weapons, ten Enfield longarms and two Whitworths. But these Whitworths were fashioned with telescopic sights. Thanks to McPhee's greed, a prying tool had been left behind. But he could not pry at the boxes and hold a brimstone match at the same time. He moved silently back to the stable area and waited for the boy to finish his chores and depart. Then he borrowed a lantern and set to work.

The first part of the plan had developed when he first saw the rifles. Without making too much noise, he was able to take four weapons at a time and hide them in the casket. And on each trip he would check on the dining salon. Preacher grinned when he saw d'Chirac lead McPhee and Donelson to a table laid out for cards. Once interested, he knew McPhee would sit at the table for hours.

He was about ready to make his last trip when there was a bumping on the side of the boat and the sound of hob-nailed boots running through the hold. He blew out the lantern and hid behind the crates.

The two sailors arrived with their own lantern and one began to work a squeaky crank. The hold cargo door began to fall outward. When it was near level, one of the rowboats came alongside.

Preacher couldn't understand their lingo, but understood their actions. They were back for a fresh supply of pitch soaked torches. That rowboat had sprung a leak and was pulled inside for later repair. A moment later a new rowboat was cranked down and departed. The two sailors who had to do the cranking began to argue. They brought up another supply of pitch torches, still screaming at each other and then seemed to agree. They took their lanterns and left.

Preacher understood their problem. Every hour, for the next eight to twelve hours, they would have to let the cargo door down to resupply the rowboats. Why not just leave it down? Which they did.

Preacher nearly roared with delight. J.T. was afraid of

having the weapons on board, so he would pleasure her. Each time he lugged a crate to the cargo door he cringed at the waste he was causing. But as each crate splashed and sank into the Mississippi, he also thought of the lives it might be saving by not getting into the hands of the guerrilla gunmen.

CHAPTER 9

BY MIDNIGHT PREACHER was annoyed, frustrated and out of sorts. The Enfield longarms and ammunition were down in the mud banks, but McPhee and Donelson were still at the card table. For his new purpose, they were now staying too long. Then he heard them stumbling down the passageway.

"The bastard!" McPhee stormed. "Just because he is losing how can he demand that the chips be left on the table until tomorrow. We won't even be here tomorrow."

"I didn't like any of it," Donelson mumbled. "Especially that damn dealing that he called a 'boot.' How am I to give you signals on my hand when he's got three damn decks of cards in that bastardly thing. It ain't fair. Wait! Someone's been in our cabin. Preacher's weapons are gone!"

"Exactly," Preacher said, silently coming up behind them with pistol in hand. "Just close the door and let's move down to the hold. Mighty interesting stuff you've ordered from d'Chirac."

"We're weaponless," McPhee wailed.

"I'm aware," Preacher said drily, "and I've got my reputation to think about. I've never yet shot a man who was unarmed. Move!"

Jarvis McPhee began to cry when he learned what Preacher had done with his new Enfield and Whitworth weapons. Donelson just looked stunned. He was fairly new to McPhee's group and took the stories about the Widow Maker to be just stories. His respect was growing by the minute, because he wanted to live. He was the first to heed Preacher's orders and got out of all his clothes, but his long johns. Then he screamed at McPhee to do the same and was helpful in putting a tie on McPhee's hands behind his back and gagging his mouth. Wordlessly, he helped Preacher push the leaking rowboat back into the river water and let his own hands be tied and a gag be put into his mouth.

Preacher shoved them off. "I'm calling you out, McPhee, for when we meet again. Don't forget that you told me why you were a great gunslinger. Your bantam legs, you said, made the other gun shoot down at you, so you could shoot up. I won't tell you my secret, you dirty bastard. You'll learn it the moment before you die. Donelson, don't ever cut my trail! The bruises you've given me will last as a memory."

The current took the rowboat downriver into darkness. There was a silent chuckle behind him and he spun.

"I've been watching you for some little time," Jacques grinned. "The makers of trouble will no longer make it."

Preacher let the breath out of his lungs slowly, then put the pistol back into his belt without taking his eyes off the French sailor. J.T. said Jacques was there to help him and he now had a job for him.

"Jacques, go to Monsier d'Chirac and your Captain. Tell them they will not have to put into Carauthersville because McPhee has just departed by rowboat with his weapons. Then, wake Madam d'Chirac and tell her the truth. I'll stay down here in the stable area until you report back."

Preacher went back to the lantern lit stalls. The lanterns had been turned low and the Mexican lad was asleep on a pallet in one of the empty stalls. The end stall was heaped with fresh hay. It smelled of home. He laid down and waited. He could feel the rhythmic beat of the paddlewheel right through the deck boards. He relaxed and let his eyes droop.

It felt so good to be lying prone that he didn't stir at various sounds. The paddlewheel began to churn slower. Rowboats bumped against the cargo door and were hauled aboard. The cargo door creaked closed and hob-nailed boots marched out of the hold. Minutes later, the engines stopped and the riverboat scraped a dock and was moored. He had no desire to investigate and would wait for Jacques to tell him why the Captain was putting into dock. He slept.

It was a marvelous dream. The spidery hand of Jean-Luc

crawling up his pant leg to entice an arousal and then using the sharp edge of her teeth to bite through the cloth and make sure she had him at full erection. Then her body was hovering over him, her lips seeking his and the warm dart of a tongue parting his lips to enter and probe. His hands came up to catch her head and return the kiss.

His hands closed around wool. The wool of a sailor cap. His eyes came open before his mind was fully awake. With one shove he got the body off of him and scrambled up. Jacques rolled out of the stall. Preacher recalled the dream and was furious, but before he could attack the man the stall area was filled with a peal of delightful laughter. The sailor rolled to a sitting position and the pom-pom topped hat came off, releasing a cascade of bountiful golden hair.

A look of surprise replaced the dangerous frown on Preacher's face. He said shortly, "I was expecting Jacques."

"But not quite in that fashion," J.T. giggled. "I couldn't help myself. God, you are a gorgeous thing to watch while you are asleep. I couldn't help myself."

"Why the charade?"

"The news of McPhee's departure has Giscard running scared. We are docked at Carauthersville because the Captain refuses to do anymore night passage now that the reason for it has departed. Giscard is so frightened of what you may have learned that he has peeked into your cabin twice since docking."

"To find an empty bunk bed? Where does he think I am?"

"In your bunk," she chuckled, taking him by the hand and leading him back to the hay mound in the stall. "Jacques is under the blankets of your bunk. Hence, how I came by his uniform and can move about the boat freely as other than myself."

"Don't you think we should return to our cabins?"

Her face mirrored her disappointment. "Not until I get what I came for."

Preacher scoffed. "I don't see any silk sheets about."

"I love the smell of hay," she cooed.

Pedro lifted from his pallet. He thought he had heard the

moan of a woman. That was impossible, he knew, because there was only one woman on board. And what a woman! Even at fourteen he knew the difference between a *putana* and a real lady. He had been a street orphan-beggar that Madame d'Chirac had rescued and brought to Lafitte's Landing as a stable groom. She was his world.

The moan came again. It had come from the next stall. He climbed the slat boards and looked down into the hay storage stall. It took a second or two to adjust his eyes to the dark of the lanternless area. For a startled, embarrassed moment, he thought he was viewing two crew members writhing in the hay. He started to scream out in disgust, when he saw that one was, indeed, a woman. The man's head and shoulders were obscured from Pedro's view by the writhing body of a woman pressing joyously down on him. He shuddered at the sight of her beautiful big breasts moving up and down in the same movement of her hips and thighs.

He didn't know why, but breasts sent his blood rushing and he remained transfixed. They hadn't noticed him, and even if they had, he was not sent away as a voyeur. Then she pulled totally off the man.

He internally gasped, for dual reasons. He was not aware a woman could moan with such pleausre over taking the length of a man in her backside. And, he was not aware a man could have such an enormous erection.

Then, as she positioned herself anew, he saw the flow of the golden hair, the profile of classic brow, nose and chin and exquisite cut of the nude body. He was viewing Madame d'Chirac with another man, but who? He didn't care. For the moment he could mentally become that man.

He watched J.T. move forward on her knees, take the huge penis and place it at the entrance of her cunt. Then she moved down on it until it had vanished. With sweat breaking out on his brow, he watched J.T. pump herself up and down on the enormous erection in faster and faster movements. He heard the man's gasp of pleasure, J.T.'s prolonged sobs. A stab of pure desire hit Pedro's stomach; for a wild moment he thought he should be with Madame d'Chirac, and in his anger, wanted the man dead.

Then, almost instantly, it was over. Preacher gave a tremendous, thrusting lurch deep inside J.T. who suddenly screamed in ecstasy, laughed outright, then fell limply on his chest.

Pedro too went limp. He had seen the man's face for the first time. This was not a common sailor, but the friendly gentleman who owned the grand horse. The pain left his stomach as did his anger, his hurt, his jealousy—everything. He felt this was a man worthy of Madame d'Chirac, because of his hatred for *Monsieur* d'Chirac.

All three heard the shuffling bedroom slippers as one.

J.T. rolled away and spied Pedro. Her thought was elsewhere.

"Giscard, damn the luck!"

Slowly, Preacher followed her gaze. J.T. had quickly got up from the hay and was standing there, gazing at Pedro, making no attempt to cover her nakedness. How odd, Pedro thought, with a strange grim, inner smile—it is the man who is embarrassed. Preacher had fumbled to find his pants to cover his groin.

A voice came out of the darkness of the hold, hard as nails. "What is going on down here?" Giscard shouted.

Pedro jumped down from his perch and ran out to ward off the man. "Going on, *Señor*? Whatever do you mean?"

"I have ears, you idiot child," d'Chirac replied in Spanish. "I heard a woman scream in sexual pleasure. Where is my wife, for she is not in her cabin?"

"*Señora* d'Chirac in the hold?" Pedro chuckled. "*Señor* is most mistaken. I am here alone with the horses."

Captain Pierre DuCorte came racing into the hold, his only desire now to salvage his vessel. "*Monsieur* Envoy, the dock is filled with armed men demanding this *Monsieur* McPhee. You will handle it, or depart my vessel!"

Wordlessly, d'Chirac brushed past him. Already, he sensed McPhee's complicity in an artfully arranged scene to embarrass him and leave him without payment for the arms.

J.T. remained quiet and aloof as Preacher began to don his clothing.

"I'm sorry," she ventured.

"Are you, J.T.?" he said icily. "Why do I have the pit of my stomach feeling that you were fully aware of what I was going to walk into?"

"He needs your help," she blustered.

"Bullshit!" he snapped. "He's wrapped in the neutral flag of France. What can they do to him?"

Jean-Luc Trauffant d'Chirac was not used to being snapped at. It shocked her into something near the truth. "They can kill him!" she snapped back. "My game is survival, and he is important, James David. I deal in favors. His life for the Whitworth rifles!"

"Oh, great," Preacher said with scorn, "I'm to take care of a dock full of guerrilla thugs with this single pistol."

She turned to the groom. "You will come with me, after I am dressed again as a sailor. *Señor* Preacher will wait here for your return and my instructions."

Preacher stood for a long moment, unsure of what he really should do next. The sailors bustling about above created a horrible echoing in the hold. Thor began to paw and snort at the unusual sound. Preacher went to pet and soothe him and cursed. He was not totally weaponless. His Whitworth was in his scabbard and ammunition in the saddlebag. He would not wait for the boy or instructions.

Five minutes earlier, or five minutes later, he might have avoided the mad scramble of sailors pouring forth from the crew quarters to take up their duty stations topside. Now their swift moving silence was eerie and frightening. They jostled him, and each other, without raising their eyes from the preparation of their weapons.

Preacher had an irrational fear that a new war was about to break out in Missouri and wasn't sure how he could help stop it. Unsure of his true position on the boat, he followed the flow of the sailors up the nearest ladder. Once on deck he collided with a short figure, was grasped by the arm, and pulled into the shadows. A voice barked at him in Spanish and he understood not a word. He was pulled along until they were next to the side rigging for the paddlewheel. The dock was ablaze with torches and Preacher could now see the face of his assailant.

Preacher started and looked at Pedro narrowly. "What the hell! Didn't I just hear J.T. speaking English with you?"

"Only for her do I use the English. Now, you are to use that ladder. At the top is a platform used to inspect and repair the paddles of the big wheel. Pronto, *señor*, for you will not need the rifle she sent."

Preacher climbed the wooden ladder and entered the wheelhouse's cool, dank interior. A section was open to the sky, with a higher platform. He crawled up and found that he could look down on the boat and the entire dock. Behind him was the wheel master and captain's cabin. He could plainly see Captain DuCorte calling down instructions to the engine room and the navigator standing ready at the wheel. Below, Giscard d'Chirac stood at one end of the gangway and a man in buckskins at the other end. Some eighteen hard faced horsemen lined the dock with rifles at the ready. They were double matched by French sailors on the main and top deck. He could hear d'Chirac lie through his teeth.

"We have no knowledge of this Jarvis McPhee, sir. We travel under the neutral flag of France and have no passengers."

"Don't lie, granpa," Lee Hartland mumbled angrily. "The boss wired from New Orleans that he and Donelson would be on this riverboat. I don't give a shit what flag you fly, jest get McPhee and our cargo off that tub!"

Preacher smiled to himself. He had not recognized the man in his buckskins attire, but the voice he would never forget. Hartland was one of McPhee's poker playing henchmen who had tried to cheat Preacher on his first visit to Missouri. With his Whitworth the man would be an easy target, but that would only bring about a bloodbath.

He looked again at d'Chirac. It was almost comical. The man was attired in a white nightshirt, slippers and nightcap equal to his mustache. But the man was so frightened that his scrawny legs were nearly buckling on him. He couldn't stand too much pressure. But as sailors and guerrilla fighters locked eyes, they did not see what Preacher was seeing. Pedro had already severed the aft mooring lines and was crawling forward. Preacher scanned the dock and the connecting street to find something to divert attention. There were no powder kegs or cotton bales to set on fire and then he spied the only possible solution.

He waited until he saw Pedro's sharp knife slice through the last strand of the hemp rope and could feel the current start to edge the boat away from the dock. He raised the rifle, aimed and fired. His accuracy was on the money. The clapper of the church bell jumped to hit the metal and sprang back to the opposite side of the cone. Preacher kept firing until the dancing clapper and fired bullets sounded like a dozen bells peeling a warning. Lights began to spring up in the town's houses.

Lee Hartland's stern look turned puzzled. McPhee's guerrilla band were not welcome in Carauthersville. He had spent the whole afternoon and evening filtering the men into town one at a time. After sundown they had captured the local marshal and locked him in one of his own cells. He now feared the man had escaped and was calling for volunteers. It was time to play hard-ball in getting the cargo and getting the hell away from the dock and town.

"Close off both ends of the dock!" he shouted. "Six of you ride up the main street and don't let anyone even think of getting this far."

He turned back to start making his demands of d'Chirac and felt something strange happening to his feet. The gangway had been slowly slipping away from its perch on the main deck and now quickly tilted and fell into the river. Hartland could not control himself or his feet. With arms waving, and mouth gaping, he slid right down the gangway into the cold February waters of the Mississippi. Nor was he seen or heard by his men, who were turning their horses to carry out his command.

It was seen by Captain DuCorte and d'Chirac. The Captain ordered the start of the engines and d'Chirac shuffled his way to the safety of the nearest passageway door.

Preacher fired three more times at the church bell, reloaded and prepared for his next target. He almost didn't get a chance to fire again. The engineer had gone from full stop to full forward. The forty-eight foot high paddle wheel

jerked with such a violent jolt that it nearly knocked Preacher
from the platform and down into the gear-teeth. He threw
out a hand to grasp the edge of the platform and dangled
dangerously. Foolishly, he was not about to let go with the
other hand of his gift rifle. The gears screamed as the steam
began to fully force them to spin the mighty weight. The next
twelve foot paddle blade began moving toward Preacher. If
his one arm was not strong enough to pull him back onto the
platform, the blade would just scrape him off his perch and
crash him down to the next blade and down into the
churning waters.

An amazing transformation took place in Preacher. The
blade became little more than a gunfighter challenging him
to the life eternal. He eyed and measured it as he would a
gunslinger's hands and holsters. He began to unbend until
he was ramrod straight and then used the rest of his strength
to swing his body to his left. His feet touched the slippery
wood and wouldn't hold. His arm felt like it was about to
pull from its socket, but he forced it to swing him right and
then left again. This time his feet took hold.

He relaxed and put his weight against the paddle bar. As it
rose it lifted him, letting the pressure off of his arm. When he
felt it was fully safe, he threw the rifle back up onto the
platform and grasped at another platform plank. Just before
the paddle came to the twelve o'clock position, he swung
back onto the narrow ledge and sat for a minute panting.

When he rose to look out the sky port the boat was forty
yards from the dock. There was confusion on both sides. The
sailors were unsure of whether they should remain at rifle
ready or take up their normal "moor lines away" duties. The
guerrilla band was split by a three way confusion. Hartland
was screaming from the icy water that he was unable to swim,
the streets were filling with armed civilians thinking the
warning a Union attack and the boat was slipping out of the
range of their old rifles. McPhee had promised them new
weapons on his return with his boat. But where was McPhee
and the weapons?

"Forget the damn boat!" Kurt Donelson shouted, taking
temporary command. "If my brother was alive on that boat

I'd hear him bellowing for us to save him. We've got to save ourselves and get out of this damn town. Fire at will!''

The ranks from each end of the dock began to ride back to join the force of six on the main street.

Those six guerrilla gunmen pulled the trigger on the most heartless, bloody chapter of the civil strife—a war within a war.

Preacher stared at the scene for a moment and then shook his head despairingly. ''Forgive me, mother, for these are now beasts of war and I am fully pulled into the war.''

From his perch he was able to swing the Whitworth right, left, right and left. The galloping lead horse fell to the street, without hearing a shot, causing the next horses to crash into them, stumble, fall, smell death and go into a panic. Then, he reduced the six street horsemen to the same level as the firing civilians. Like every bully with their advantage taken away, they turned and fled back to their comrades who were rapidly becoming no better off.

With their avenue of escape all but closed, Preacher returned his aim to the church bell clapper. It rang when the boat was 500 yards, a 1000 yards and 2000 yards from the dock. It rang even as moving paddle after moving paddle dashed Preacher with a chilly spray of cold water.

Because the church deacon never touched hand on rope to ring the warning bell, the people of Carauthersville held it as a message from God.

Preacher was only human, and a frustrated one at that, taking it out on the bell. He had learned two things the time he had bedded Betsy Fuller. First, that part of his destiny in life was to be a man who could fully pleasure women and be fully pleasured in return. Secondly, that women could use the sexual act, or denial of it, as a most powerful weapon to sate their desires.

He came down out of the wheel housing feeling fully betrayed by J.T.

He thought the cold water from the paddle wheel had calmed him until he turned into the passageway. He became increasingly irritated at the welcoming committee standing by nearly every open door.

"Dear boy," d'Chirac smirked, "how can I—"

Preacher marched by without looking at him.

J.T. looked shocked, standing in the doorway to the White Suite. "You don't fully understand what I have done for you—"

He walked on without letting her finish.

Jacques stood attention erect, his eyes a mixture of respect and hatred.

Pedro stood at the open door of his cabin. "I brought dry clothing up from your saddlebag, *señor.*"

He nodded and entered. The door slammed behind him. He sighed, thankful to be alone. But when he turned, he stared into eyes that were hardly of a peaceful nature.

"You have been cruel, *señor,*" Pedro said hotly. "Madam d'Chirac is not a wanton *putana* who would use her body to the fullest to lure a man!"

Preacher crossed his arms and closed his eyes. "You are hardly an expert on that subject, unless she has already measured your young stick."

"Never!" he repeated, almost sadly. "I am on this journey to be given to you as a gift."

"No way," Preacher cried. "She knows me better than that!"

Pedro would not relent. "You take my words all wrong, even though she found me in that life in Mexico. My uncles sold me to the highest French bidders. She had *Señor* d'Chirac bid highest and bring me to LaFitte's Landing. Now I am to be yours."

"Why?" Preacher moaned. "I am no officer in need of an aide or lackey."

"Nor with knowledge of this weapon," he said softly.

Preacher's back stiffened. "I've done fine with it so far."

"Yes, you have," the youth mused, as though an elder. "Using it like another rifle, and badly."

Preacher smirked. "And you are an expert, at your age?"

Preacher caught a sudden, smoldering look in Pedro's eyes. He had been wrong to equate it to age, for not that many years separated them and times were changing very rapidly.

"Quite," Pedro said gravely. "I made myself an expert in such matters, because my uncles were arms importers and could not figure out how the elements fit together or the proper grain weight for each bullet. They began to hate my knowledge, rather than use it. Why do some men think that boys cannot do manly tasks?''

Preacher found himself laughing. ''I know that position fully, Pedro. I wonder, though, if you are willing to pay the price of growing up too fast.''

''It is my fate,'' he said gravely. ''Now I must see to other chores.''

Preacher was bone weary. He tugged off the wet clothing and crawled into the bunk bed. Somehow he knew he would not be disturbed.

CHAPTER 10

NOR WAS HE disturbed for the next two days. He was not locked in, but still felt like a prisoner.

Pedro brought his food and twice each day would take him onto the fantail and teach him all the wonders of the Whitworth. His fascination grew over the weapon with the telescopic sighting piece. He could clearly aim at an object over 5,000 feet upriver and have to wait for the riverboat to travel that mile to view that he had hit his target. A mile! He could make a bullet travel a mile faster than any other bullet known and be accurate! His mind raced.

Reality returned on their arrival at Cairo, Illinois. A troop of well armed Union soldiers came on board to give the Envoy a safe journey to his meeting in Paducah, Kentucky. Paducah was just 25 miles eastward up the Ohio river and controlled the exits of the Tennessee and Cumberland as they flowed into the Ohio. At Paducah, Preacher saw the growing might of Halleck's Army of Ohio. Tents stretched for miles and blue clad soldiers huddled around bonfires.

As soon as the Jean-Luc was docked, Jacques came to take Preacher to the main deck. It was quite a scene. Six sailors stood at attention around the flower topped casket. Two men in funeral parlor garb stood waiting. Pedro was leading Thor and the other two horses from the cargo ramp and onto a flatboat barge bedecked in black crepe. At the head of the casket, J.T. sat in mourning black.

Stoically, she rose and handed Preacher a piece of black cloth.

"What in the hell is this for?"

J.T. chuckled deep within her throat. "To face the problem we face, J.D., a certain amount of levity is useful. Put on the mourning band. Death is like a flag of truce in wartime. The funeral director is really an old friend of Sam Cook's. His funeral barge will take you to Luden's Dock, which is a mile below Fort Donelson. Both the Union and Confederate sides have been advised. Because of your deep grief, they are aware a family retainer is along to see to your needs."

She hesitated. "In my Creole world we look at life as single steps, some good and some bad. You came to me for assistance. I'm unsure if my step was good or bad. We cannot part on bad terms."

But the terms were her terms, Preacher thought cynically. And yet, why send Pedro with him? That was really for his protection and knowledge of the weapons. Instantly he recognized that she was doing much for him, but had to appear as safeguarding her husband, if only in name.

"You have reason to stand proud, my young warrior," she whispered.

"You are one of the loveliest women I have ever beheld."

"We shall still burn a city down with our love," she chuckled.

He stood and let his eyes absorb every portion of her body; then he slowly turned and went onto the dock and toward the flat-boat. The casket followed.

J.T. stood benumbed and confused. She had longed for a kiss of forgiveness. With trembling hands she let Jacques escort her back to her cabin. Then she laughed. When would she ever learn that Preacher played his various roles in life better than an actor on a stage. Still, she dreaded how long it might be before they were together again. He had a mystical quality over her. She could sense his needs before they were presented.

It was the one reason she had looked at Pedro Duarte and declared: "I know a man who can elevate you to your true worth on this planet."

Preacher played the grieving relative, but kept his eyes and ears alert. At Hamlesburg the Union gunboats, which had attacked Fort Donelson, were docked. The Luden funeral

director put into port more for information than the awaiting
food. Purposely, he had squeezed between two of the gunboats. Nor was the surplus food by happenstance. Coming
downstream that morning he had stopped and left a message
for his sister-in-law at Hamlesburg.

"Maggie, you are the goddess of a man's hunger dreams.
Hey, you Yankee boys, Maggie makes the best fried chicken
in Tennessee. Come get some hot vittles."

"Don't seem proper."

"Proper?" Horace Luden chortled. "This was a right
proper Irish lady. We gave her husband a wake that lasted for
days. She won't rest easy in heaven without proper eating and
laughter about her."

Preacher was impressed. The Ludens, father and son, were
expert hosts and intelligence gathering ears. Fort Donelson
had been under siege for ten days. General Grant had been
trying to gain more forces, but the return of the Fort Henry
soldiers had each side nearly even at 15,000. But the main
concern for the gunboat sailors was for Commodore Andrew
Foote. During the battle for Fort Donelson, Foote had been
badly wounded by rifle fire when they were far out of range of
any Confederate riflemen. Every Union rifleman on ship and
shore was under suspicion and it had the morale very low.

As a result, gunboat riflemen had been ordered to over-
shoot, sending their shells howling harmlessly over the object
of their deadly aim.

The next shock for Preacher was passing beneath the
ramparts of Fort Donelson. The east and northwest banks of
the river were still Union camps, but quiet and forlorn.
Winter warfare was taking its toll. He could almost see their
uniformed bodies shiver over the thought of how much
longer the siege could continue. The fort, on its high bluff,
was like a gray painting of a deathly hell. No movement. No
signal to acknowledge them. Silence.

Luden's Dock was like coming from night to dawn. All
seventy-two of the souls who inhabited the area were on hand
to welcome the barge and help get the casket to the small
cemetery overlooking the Mississippi River. As though pre-
trained, they surrounded the burial plot for the rifles to be
taken from the casket and put into bundles for the extra horse

to carry. Then they vanished, leaving Preacher, Pedro and the Luden funeral men.

Pedro brought saddlebags from the extra horses and began putting them into the open casket.

"What's this?" Preacher demanded.

"Orders from Madam d'Chirac. It is the gold payment from Senor McPhee for the weapons. The cost of your weapons has already been deducted and given to her husband.Some, by her instructions, have been put into your saddlebags to see to my pitiful salary. Need I say more?"

"Hardly," Preacher said sourly. "Close the casket and let it drop. I will help fill it in."

Later, as they wound their way up the turning bluff roads back to Fort Donelson, Preacher asked, "Pedro, what did we just bury at that site?"

Pedro didn't flinch. "According to Madam d'Chirac, more than $20,000 in gold coin."

Preacher whistled. "Quite a bounty to have on my head, for McPhee will search me out for its hiding place."

He soon learned that others were searching him out.

Preacher had no idea who the visitor might be with General Forrest. He had been given orders to report back directly to General Forrest and that is exactly what he had done but this man had been insultingly rude.

"I beg your pardon," Preacher stammered. "I was only following your orders."

"Orders, hmmph," Nate Forrest clucked good naturedly. "Sorry, Captain Huntington, that I misused a messenger from the Virginia Command."

"I humbly accept your apology," Prescott Huntington sneered, in an arrogant tone.

"Would someone please tell me what is going on?" Morgan Lake demanded.

Obediently, if thoughtlessly, Brent Barrett cut through the tangle of words. "It would seem that we used this lad for our mission, while, indeed he bore information for General Pillow. According to Captain Huntington, he is charged with high treason."

Preacher's legs almost gave out on him. The news so

stunned him, he sat down heavily, military or not.

"Which is pure rubbish," Morgan Lake stormed. "General, don't ruin your command with a lie of your own. Who let General Pillow know Preacher was back?"

"I could not lie to Captain Huntington," Forrest quickly accepted, "for they spotted him floating by the fort on a funeral barge. He is to report at once."

They were all looking at Preacher, and seemed embarrassed.

Slowly Preacher lifted his head. "Well," he said mustering a smile. "I'm recognized at any rate. Will someone take care of Pedro while I go with Captain Huntington as a prisoner."

Preacher had made it a form of challenge. It fell on silence. But, because no one moved to take away his brace of pistols or saddle scabbard, he left quietly, but dubiously.

"He will hate me forever," Forrest sighed.

"Not when he learns the truth," Brent Barrett said. "He is youthful and will forgive your lie."

"Which was unnecessary!" Morgan Lake stormed. "Damn, he is back, two days short of challenge. The traitor is among us who let the fort know who he was and when he came back. Are you blind to that?"

Nathan Bredford Forrest hung his head and grinned. "Hardly, my brilliant Colonel. To smoke out that traitor needed a rabbit in the trap. My regard for Preacher is paramount, but worthless if he knew I loved him while throwing him to the wolves. He had to hate me, think I had turned against him. Then, and only then, will he give Pillow a true picture of what they are up against. They say my agents lie. If they thought he was still my agent, they would say the same. Now they will accept his words as truth.

"Now, as for you, my young friend brought by the Preacherman. Do I speak Spanish or English? Do I get answers or abuse?"

Pedro bowed deeply toward him in traditional Spanish style and then rose and laughed in his face. "Your gringo questions are many and cannot be answered simply no or yes. I make, therefore, a statement. I am a free citizen of Mexico, which is under the neutral flag of France, here to serve freely, a dear friend, *señor* J.D. Preacher. I say no more."

"What of the weapons?" Forrest demanded.

Pedro was helpless to aid them until they aided Preacher. Returning to the horses, he saw a large drunken man approaching them with no reason. A lamp from a tent shone on a metal piece in the man's hand and he realized the dangerous situation facing the horses.

Like a jungle cat stalking its night prey, Pedro skittered around to the back of the nearest tent. He stopped only once to check on his own knife and length of Mexican leather thong.

The camp was deathly still. A lone night owl screeched far off. Pedro slid along a tent wall toward the tethered horses.

Then he was close enough to hear that the drunken man was not alone.

"You can drop the drunk act, Kirt. It so happens that Huntington has already come for Preacher. That was an idiot act calling out that you recognized him on the flatboat."

Kirtland McPhee clawed at his mustache and regarded Lieutenant Paul Cousins with a fierce glare.

"I said," Cousins began again, "that—"

"I heard you!" Kirt snarled. "Don't be telling me my job."

"Then don't lie to me," the short, stocky man said flatly. "Your Uncle Jarvis wired us to get back his weapons and gold."

"And I went upstream to find the funeral barge and track them back here. The weapons are bundled on these two horses and I'm sure the gold is in his saddlebags. Now, let's get the hell out of here."

"We can't!" he spat. "I was to call Preacher out and kill him."

"Then why in the hell did you let them take him to the fort?"

"Oh, you blind, simple fool! The only reason we are here is to keep track of Morgan Lake and make sure that Forrest's Raiders do not come back into Missouri. I've killed two signal men, just so I would be the lone signal officer for this outfit. Every time we get a message about a guerrilla raid in Missouri, it mysteriously vanishes. That's our main worth to your uncle. Don't screw things up."

"Stay if you want, but I've got a boatman at Hamlesberg who will take me and the weapons back to Missouri."

Cousins started to protest, but Kirt brought his pistol quickly from his holster, flipped it and caught the young officer squarely on the side of the head with the butt. The blow was so sudden, catching Cousins so unaware, that he had only a moment of vision before he blacked out and went sprawling on the ground.

In an instant, Pedro came flying from the darkness, leaped into the air and came down jamming his feet through Kirt's legs, flipping him off balance. Pedro jumped away, spun and jumped again to come down on the sprawling man's arm and wrist. Kirt let out a howl and loosened his grip on the weapon. Pedro kicked it away as Kirt leaped frantically to his feet and stood for a moment in total puzzlement, his huge body trembling with rage.

"You're that damn Mex traveling with Preacher," he growled.

Pedro was smart enough to know the big man could break him in two, if given the chance. He needed help and figured out the quickest way of getting it.

"Horse thief! Horse thief! Horse thief!"

Kirtland McPhee's lower jaw dropped.

Within seconds they were surrounded by men, including Morgan Lake and Brent Barrett. Kirt's arms were immediately pinned behind his back and an attempt was made to revive Cousins.

"Why, he's the messenger from the fort to our signal officer. Cousins must have figured out he was the one who let the fort know about Preacher and challenged him. Who are you?"

Kirt was not about to speak. Let them believe that version.

"Pedro," Morgan demanded, "what did you see and hear?"

Pedro felt uncomfortable. He had heard much, but his English was so limited that he had not been able to grasp all of their fast talk. Only Preacher would be able to make sense out of the bits and pieces he could recall. "He wished to steal our horses and weapons," he said simply.

"Get him out of here and up to the fort," Morgan growled. "Put a guard on these horses. Farraday, you speak Spanish. Take the lad to the mess tent and see if you can learn anymore. Bring Cousins around and bring him to me. I will personally take him to report to General Pillow.''

General Gideon Pillow apparently had a mania for isolation, which disturbed his equal in command, General John Floyd. They kept separate offices and quarters on opposite sides of the fort. Foot messengers were constantly crossing paths with each other. Major Reeves Bruster, the signal officer, had jokingly suggested carrier pigeons at either end of the fort. They would have been a great help on the night of February 13, 1862.

John Floyd was perplexed. Huntington had taken Preacher first to General Pillow, who sent him back to Floyd.

''We use spies occasionally in war time, you know,'' he said to Huntington, smiling. ''Gideon was even a spy for Polk in Mexico. But treason? You've heard his report to General Pillow and now myself. Where is the treason?''

Huntington was uncomfortable. He was caught between two superior officers who openly hated each other. ''A firing squad does seem harsh, sir. But you do know General Pillow and how he goes into seclusion once he's given orders. He's retired for the night.''

For John Floyd that was not satisfactory. According to the report, this soldier had been sent there through an indirect, though high priority, chain of command. But no one had knowledge of the original source of his orders nor why he was there.

''The only thing I see, Huntington, is that he was given different orders by General Forrest, who is not really under our command. The lad seems to have taken that matter in hand and got the job done.''

''To fool us, perhaps?'' Huntington sneered. ''On my own, sir, I checked with the Virginia command. They have no record of a James David Preacher. The nearest name was a J.D. Preacher. His last commander was a personal friend, Major Randolph Newberry. That man was sent to us, but was untrainable and did not know weaponry. Hardly the same man, if you ask me.''

General Floyd did not wish to ask Preacher questions in front of the insufferable young captain, whom he had marked in his mind as a spy for General Pillow. ''Leave the

lad with me, Captain Huntington, I want to ponder this and
then ask him a few more questions.''

Huntington saluted, left Preacher sitting in the General's
anteroom and went out into the cold night air. Even though
it was just a little after eight o'clock it seemed like midnight.
He went to the Signal Corps cabin to find Lance Corporal
Kirtland McPhee. He had an urgent message to send to
Lieutenant Paul Cousins. A fake message had to be prepared
to make the redoubtable Nathan Bedford Forrest look black.

Huntington found nothing but an empty cabin. He started
toward the barracks when a guard opened a side gate to the
fort. Kirt McPhee was shoved through the opening, his hands
tied behind him, and the sentry told to put the man down in
a stockade cell. Huntington started forward to countermand
the order when General Floyd stepped into the court and
started across to General Pillow's quarters. Huntington
pulled into the shadows and waited. He thought Floyd an
idiot to take Preacher back to Pillow.

The path of the two prisoners passed. They did not
exchange looks, but were quite aware of each other and how
they could affect each other's lives.

Ironically, it was Preacher who grinned. Only someone
from Missouri could have recognized him on that barge and
the last time he had seen Kirt McPhee was at the rebuilt farm
near Martinstown Farm. He had stood shotgun over his uncle
while Jarvis McPhee had counted out slave papers for Preacher
to take to the Johnston's farm. Preacher was glad Kirt was
there and guessed he was the one who had revealed him. He
had a score to settle and that would just make it easier. That
was, if he could settle his own score. He didn't like Pillow's
order for a firing squad.

''Hope I didn't wake you, Gideon,'' lied Floyd.

''What brings you over here? News of the siege, I hope.''

Floyd settled himself grimly on the cot—the only other
place to sit besides Gideon's field desk chair—while the gray-
whiskered general huddled over a charcoal brazier. Preacher
stood in the door of the little headquarters room, totally
ignored.

''No,'' he said, shaking his head, ''nothing on the siege,
and yet it is. We can't get any intelligence on Grant's

movements, but have someone who has just come upstream.
I think we need to listen to the Preacher lad—''

''No!''

''Yes! He has the knowledge that we are desperate to
learn.''

''How can we trust him?''

''Gideon, Gideon, Gideon,'' said Floyd softly. ''If Nate
Forrest trusts him—''

''Which I don't,'' Pillow barked. ''I've decided to ask for a
new cavalry unit to replace that worthless crew.''

Preacher jumped in like a mother tiger. ''The hell you
say!'' he roared. ''Not after what I've been through for them.
Now I know what they said in Virginia was true about you.
They said you would let this U.S. Grant march right up to
within gunshot of any entrenchments you were given to hold.
It has happened. Morgan Lake taught me to read battle
standards when I was with the Missouri militia. Do you really
know what you are facing?''

''Quite!'' Pillow stormed. ''Just enough to hold us under
siege. Henry Halleck has the main forces warm and safe up
Paducah way. I know my enemy, you young rabble rouser.
Halleck is a large emptiness surrounded by an education. He
is too ambitious to attack.''

''Because of no need,'' Preacher said bitterly. ''But you are
partially right, General. There are more tents around
Paducah than I've seen in my life. Several divisions, but they
are there for the protection of the French Envoy who is
meeting with Halleck as President Lincoln's envoy. France
will stay out of the war, on both sides. As France goes, so goes
Mexico.''

Pillow was startled by Preacher's explosive defense of the
situation, and somewhat hurt by Floyd letting him go on. But
the news of that meeting really shocked him. Under very
secret orders from President Jefferson Davis, he had quietly
sent General Simon Bolivar Buckner to attend on behalf of
the Confederate State of America. It was his main reason for
sitting up that night. Buckner was to have returned late that
night or early the next morning. He decided to listen more
carefully for the moment.

''But won't Grant need that help?'' he asked. ''After all,

we have the Fort Henry troops back and are nearly at 15,000 men. What does Grant have?"

"I can only report on what I saw, Sir. The naval force has grown and commands the river. When was the last time you saw a riverboat dare come downstream from Nashville? But, from the barge I was able to see your landward rear and flanks. On the right was a division and general staff standard. Behind you, stretching back to Fort Henry, is the division standard I saw when I left. But now, to the left is a third division and general staff standard. I'm new to war, sir, but not to counting. Grant may have pulled some forces during the siege, but quietly replaced them."

Pillow paled until his face and whiskers were of equal color. "Can he be correct?" He still found it hard to believe.

"I find truth in his words, although it scares the hell out of me."

"Still, we will check his report against Buckner's report to headquarters."

"We can't wait to hear back from Richmond, Gideon."

"John," Pillow said, as though talking to a naughty boy, "this is headquarters. You're sitting in it. Now, I would like a cat-nap until Simon returns."

Floyd accepted the inevitable gracefully, although he didn't understand where General Buckner might be. For the moment he had the Preacher lad off the hook and quietly motioned him away.

A shivering Morgan Lake and Paul Cousins met them outside Pillow's quarters. With a warning look from Preacher, Morgan quickly decided to report the Kirt McPhee incident to General Floyd.

"Ah, yes, the man we saw them bring in. Let's not rattle General Pillow's mind with a new matter. Your young Preacher has just rattled his mind quite enough. Cousins, go to the infirmary and have them see to your head. Colonel Lake, I must keep Preacher here for the night, but would like to see you and General Forrest tomorrow afternoon."

Lake whispered quickly to Preacher. "What about Pedro? He won't talk or eat without you."

"Tell him you are the Morgan Lake who taught me to shoot. I've told him the story."

"What if he doesn't believe me?"

"Show him your cross draw. He'll believe that."

"Damn it, Preacher. Every time you cut my trail I find myself in a different soup. Will it never end?"

"Nope," Preacher chuckled. "The teacher is now by pupil taught."

He took a single saddlebag from Thor and went to the barracks that the General had indicated. Oddly, he recalled it was the same barracks to which they had taken Kirt McPhee. It was a cavernous, drafty log structure which wouldn't hold the heat from the two pot-bellied stoves.

A Sergeant came up to him suspiciously.

"You supposed to be down in the cells?"

Preacher shook his head and the guard moved off, watchful. Preacher noted that behind him was a pit opening and wooden ladder. He dropped his saddlebag and squatted Indian fashion, quietly taking his brace of pistols out and hiding them under his thighs. He felt uneasy with Kirt McPhee around, even if he was a prisoner.

When his eyes adjusted to the gloom he looked about. Some fifty to sixty men sat huddled under shoulder wrapped blankets. He looked from face to face and they stared back at him curiously or blankly or averted their eyes. No one raised a hand in greeting or spoke. It was eerie. The eyes he had seen before, too many times. The eyes of men who knew they would soon be dead.

Then a figure approached the Sergeant and something was slipped from one hand to the other. The Sergeant departed the barracks and the figure went to the pit opening. As he stepped onto the wooden ladder, the lantern light from below caught his face. It was the same officer Preacher had seen sent to the infirmary. He wished now he had questioned Morgan about the man. He crawled to the pit and heard whispered murmurs. He strained his ears to hear what was said. It was drowned out by a strident call from the Sergeant outside the barracks.

"Prisoner escape! Prisoner escape! Man the walls and portals."

Preacher moved into the pit before he was fully aware of what had possessed him. Something smelled and he didn't like it.

In the underground pit were three cells, little more than 5 by 5 by 5 dungeons. All were empty, except one. In that cell the officer was smashing his fist again and again into McPhee's body and head. "You won't ruin me," Cousins wailed. "You won't!"

Kirt McPhee could not fight back. His hands and feet were firmly bound. Through his haze of frozen terror, he saw the figure drop into the pit. Only one man alive could cast a shadow like that on the sandstone wall. He shouted angrily. "He's in this, too, Preacher. That's why he wants me dead and silent."

Cousins spun, crouched, petrified. "We are under orders from Jarvis McPhee."

"Untie his ropes, Lieutenant," ordered Preacher grimly. "There's only one way that son-of-a-bitch can properly escape." He took the pistols from his holsters and started toward them. He had to crouch down nearly a foot, but didn't take his eyes off of them.

"You don't shoot unarmed men."

"That's right," Preacher chuckled, "but I'm not responsible for sentries on the wall shooting escaping prisoners. Move, McPhee! In one second lead is going to start climbing that ladder. You best be one rung ahead of each shot."

McPhee ran. With fascinated disbelief Cousins watched the bullets chewing into the pit wall, spitting out bits of sandstone between each ladder rung. Kirt jumped from rung to rung and vanished.

Preacher reholstered cross-handed, confusing Cousins. Which had been the gun that had fired, which had not? Then, the fear that had galvanized him evaporated. He stopped trembling and felt exultant. This man was no great gunslinger. He was a novice. An idiot. He had holstered his weapons and now had turned his back on him and in a crouching walk was going back to the pit ladder. It was just going to be too easy. No one would blame him for shooting a man in the back who had just helped a prisoner escape. And, like Preacher, he knew Kirt would never get by the alerted guards. He also saw the glory he would gain in having brought down the Widow Maker.

Paul Cousins made it okay to the drawing and quick cock of the gun, and then he froze. He clutched his heart at the sudden burning sensation that wouldn't go away. Then he saw Preacher, before his eyes saw no more.

Preacher got up from his half turned, crouch position. "Poor dumb sap," he muttered. "They kept me in the Virginia command long enough to learn I don't have to watch their eyes. The cheap Argentine leather they buy for holsters squeaks when you pull iron. Don't pull a gun on Preacher's back, when he's got ears."

Kirt McPhee stared down into the pit with feelings compounded of hatred and respect for what he had heard, and of admiration—even affection—he would have denied. But what if Cousins had killed the gunslinger? Then this very minute he, Kirt McPhee, would have been forced to kill Cousins. But he didn't want a further run in with Preacher. Because this was his normal barracks, he crawled to his spot and covered himself with his blanket.

The most confused individual of all was Sergeant Odell. The Officer-of-the-Guard had him stammering in confusion.

"Captain," Preacher said, soothingly, "let's put things back into their logical order. The Lieutenant came and ordered the Sergeant to let him go down to the prisoner. It was the Lieutenant who called up for the Sergeant to warn the sentries that the prisoner was trying to escape. It was then that I jumped down in the pit and found the Lieutenant trying to strangle and beat up on the prisoner. When I broke that up, the prisoner did escape. You know the result of our shootout."

The officer looked at Odell strangely, and Odell looked saintly.

"What was that all about?" Odell whispered, when they were alone.

"I saw you take the money," Preacher said candidly. "And I know McPhee never left this barracks, because in that pit you can hear every footstep. Find him and make sure he properly escapes."

"Why?"

"Let's just say he has a destiny with Preacher's law. Now, how many years do you get for taking a bribe?"

Odell turned away, a look of ugly, angry pain on his face.

By midnight he was grinning again. His eight p.m. and eleven p.m. barracks headcount was off by one. He knew at once the reason and determined under which blanket. Quietly, he got McPhee out of the barracks and to a spot for easy escape. But, because his war career had been built upon receiving bribes, he demanded again. Kirt McPhee countered, only if he had a pistol and a bowie knife. The price went double and McPhee agreed.

At dawn, Preacher was roused from a frozen sleep. He was taken to an escape door on the west wall of the fort and confronted by the same guard officer of the night before.

"What do you make of that?"

Preacher looked anxiously from the Captain to the prone figure. "I make it to be a man with his throat slit from ear to ear."

"Bastard!" Captain Rogers growled his frustrated hatred of gentlemen soldiers. He had won his rank on the field of battle in Mexico and switched his uniforms when his beloved Mississippi entered the war. "You lied last night about the prisoner and now he lies dead and with his purse strings cut. General Pillow does not trust you, nor do I. You are under house arrest."

Preacher shrugged indifferently. In the milling crowd of soldiers he had seen a familiar brown face.

Pedro turned and shuffled his feet in the dust. He had just come with a message for Preacher and would have to return to Morgan Lake with a conflicting message. He did not think he liked America. Even in Mexico, under a harsh French puppet Emperor, there seemed to be more justice.

Preacher accepted it with controlled amusement. Once again he had not been denied his weapons and if necessary, could have shot his way to freedom.

Nate Forrest came alone to the fort on the afternoon of February 14. Farraday had gotten through to the Mexican lad and Morgan Lake and Pedro had two dozen men upstream learning to use the Whitworth rifles.

In the officer's mess, Forrest followed with interest the debriefing of General Buckner. They stood around a table on which the terrain map lay. He seemed embarrassed and reluctant in his role of informer, though he had apparently performed it well.

"Even in front of Ambassador d'Chirac, Halleck was quite open on his hatred of Grant. He boasted that this operation would be Union successful because of the generals he has put down here. McClernand, Wallace and C.F. Smith."

"Good heavens?" said Pillow incredulously. "John McClernand I might question, because he is a politically appointed general, but Lew Wallace won his fame as a great field officer in Mexico and salty old C.F. Smith even I respected when he was Commandant of Cadets at West Point."

"They are not your real problem, gentlemen. Even as I was leaving Paducah, river barges were loading reinforcements. By tomorrow, Grant will have an additional 10,000 troops."

Floyd took Pillow aside. "Understand, Gideon, if we are captured by such a force they will look on us quite differently. Halleck detests me for having weakened the Federal strike force while Secretary of War. Will Grant let your neck stay its same length for all you did to him?"

Pillow hurried back to the terrain map in embarrassment. Even though he agreed with John Floyd, he could not show it in word or action.

"Gentlemen, General Floyd has just asked that we consider this meeting a counsel of war. I fully agree. Sentry, close the door and see that we are not disturbed."

Word spread like wildfire that something was afoot. The sun set blood red. A cold snap out of Canada dropped the temperature to below zero. The Union soldiers shivered on their arms, the Rebels huddled together in the fort warmed by the thought that the counsel of war stretched on into the night.

Six times Preacher was called to the meeting to restate what he had seen and the military placements he could recall. Oddly, on his last visit, he was not excused.

"So," Pillow sighed. "We are agreed on a breakout and escape. From what we have learned from Private Preacher, their right flank seems the most disorganized. Buckner, before dawn quietly get a column into the entrenchments. The fort guns will hold back their gunboats. Forrest, you will then bring up the cavalry.''

"Shouldn't the cavalry make the first charge, General?" Forrest stated.

"So far I've seen no evidence to support the fact that they are cavalry, General Forrest. What have you done of late?''

"Wait for orders.''

"And another thing, Forrest," Pillow rapped out angrily. "Rifles are an infantry weapon, not cavalry. Those rifles smuggled to you by Preacher will be brought to me, at once. I wish to see if the gunnery officer's story of its power is correct.''

"General . . .'' Preacher started slowly. "It is true you are the Commanding Officer and can order such, but, sir, the attack is for tomorrow. This isn't the manner of weapon you put into untrained hands.''

Pillow smiled at him from behind the terrain map, but it wasn't a friendly smile. "I have come to start trusting your word, Private. So be it that we do not have time to train men on the weapons. However, you will stay with me on the ramparts with your weapon.''

"As you command," muttered Preacher in disgust. He had expected Nate Forrest to speak up and ask for his assignment to the cavalry. The man was silent, with a problem of his own. He totally disagreed with the battle plan, but could say no more.

Chapter 11

THEY CAME OUT of the entrenchment at dawn in a long line of gray and butternut. Two thousand marched toward the unsuspecting Yankees. From the rampart Preacher could look down into the fort where nine thousand waited, rifles primed and ready. As yet, he had not seen a sign of Forrest's Raiders and it made him wonder.

When the Rebs came upon McClernand's camp, there was no mad dash of running, yelling infantrymen. They swept into the camp like a swarm of locusts going through a grain field. The Yankees buried themselves under the supply wagons as a tortoise hides in its carapace.

The cannon boomed in the direction of the gunboats, but their shells fell short into the water.

"They're afraid to get any closer," Pillow chortled.

" 'Fraid not, General," Preacher muttered, taking his eye away from his telescopic-sighted Whitworth. "They're waiting to convoy two other gunboats and the barges they are towing."

"What in the hell are you talking about? I see nothing."

With a grin Preacher pointed downstream and handed him the weapon. Clumsily, Pillow put it to his eye, squinted, frowned, peered downstream again and then back into the telescope.

"Little difference," he shrugged. "They are barely making headway against the current."

Preacher took the rifle back. "True. Even though this first attack is driving the Feds back, won't they take heart when

they see those barges? I think I could slow them down more
and cause some confusion.''

"Hop to it then, boy," ordered Pillow coldly. He turned
on the rampart stiffly and pointed to the battlefield. "And
where in the damn hell is my cavalry?"

Preacher couldn't have cared less. His interest was in the
gunboats and the manner in which they were towing the
barges. Tether lines went out to six barges each. In their vee
formation, the helmsmen were having to fight their rudder to
keep in position and not crash into another barge. Preacher
looked on them like a flight of geese. Cause problem to the
leader, and the others would panic and be easy prey.

The first rudderman went into the water so silently, the
hundred soldiers on his barge never looked back. The same
was true of the rudderman on the lead barge of the second
gunboat. The barges began to drift over the lines of the
following barges. One sailor, in charge of the lines on a
gunboat, started to shout a warning. Preacher made sure the
warning stayed in his throat.

Several shots later, not a single rudderman was left on a
flatboat. Barges drifted and bumped, and lines became
entangled. The soldiers became aware that something weird
was happening, but were unsure of what to do to correct it.
Gunboat crewmen were frantically trying to pull in the lines
to bring the barges close.

Preacher spared their lives and fired at the hemp lines.
Because they were taut from the strain, the bullets quickly
snapped the last strands. Free, the barges began to circle with
the current, around and around. The soldiers began to panic,
jump overboard and swim to shore. Many, upon hitting the
water, realized they didn't know how to swim. They
screamed, flailed at thin air and went under.

One gunboat Captain ordered a mid-river turning to try
and recapture his barges. Preacher saw the gunboat start to
turn and sighted on the wheelhouse. The helmsman grabbed
at the turning wheel and froze. The wheel froze with him.
Before his Captain could react, his iron-plated bow was
knifing into the mid-section of the other gunboat. Its boiler
exploded, enveloping both in a cloud of hissing steam.

After two hours of hard fighting, infantry and cavalry had made a wide, if somewhat bloody, escape route between Fort Donelson and the river. Buckner swept his brigade into a rear-guard position to protect the getaway.

"Gunboat coming at full steam, General."

"Shall I send another unit into the entreachment?"

"Colonel Ferris wants to know if he should start the escape march?"

"Wallace's division is being moved in to help. Shall we prepare for another attack?"

Pillow stood confused. Floyd was nowhere in sight. He hesitated, answering no questions for the moment.

Preacher had been watching the advance of the gunboat through the telescope. On the bridge was a dumpy general officer, chopping on a cigar. His face was white with fear. Grant had been downstream conferring with the wounded Commodore Foote when he got news of the battle. Preacher saw him crush the papers he held in his hand and bark at a Navy signalman.

"What's he saying?" Preacher asked Major Buster and handed him the rifle.

"General Pillow, that's Grant. He's giving orders to Wallace that the right must be retaken to make sure that the escape door is shut. He's ordering General Smith to come around and attack with his whole division, every damn regiment. General?"

He turned. He and Preacher were standing alone on the rampart.

"What do I do?" Preacher asked.

"Nothing, until I find them and get orders."

Only later, in another battle, would Preacher realize that the tide of the entire war was in his sights. Later, the Whitworth would be used to deprive Union forces of their leadership by singling out officers for their targets. But, for the moment, it was Fort Donelson that was leaderless.

Into the afternoon and evening, Preacher was left alone on the rampart. He saw the cavalry mysteriously melt back into the woods. He watched as Buckner's brigade was driven back to the entrenchments and fort proper. At sunrise, they had been a force of 15,000. At sunset, 11,500 frightened men huddled in the fort. He didn't even want to contemplate the bodies U.S. Grant was counting.

It was a strange counsel of war. Two Generals, three Colonels and a Major.

Buckner was near tears. "Pillow, Floyd and their personal command staff vanished during the afternoon. I am senior in command. Do you read me clearly?"

One "Yes, sir!" assured him of no problem from Forrest.

"All right," he gulped. "I sent a note to General Grant for surrender terms, for we are doomed men. This is the answer, which I find ungenerous and unchivalrous. 'No terms except an unconditional and immediate surrender can be accepted. I propose to move immediately upon your works.' "

"Harsh, indeed," Buster fumed, "because he thinks we harbor Pillow and Floyd. Odd, it just struck me that *unconditional surrender* fit his initials. Have we any other choice, gentlemen? A fort, 11,500 men and all their equipment. The most damaging blow of the war against the Confederacy."

Nathan Bedford Forrest turned to leave.

"General?"

"I go to inform my men."

Outside the officers' mess, because the door had been left open, Preacher heard it all. Nate Forrest rushed by him as though the devil was on his tail. Preacher waited a few minutes and then went for Thor. He was in no mood to surrender to anyone. If big time Generals could vanish, so could he. But, foolishly, he felt an obligation to J.T. He would have to go get Pedro and take him to safety.

The news spread through the cavalry tents with shocking speed. The men crowded around Forrest, stunned and seeking reassurance. Their insistent questions grew into an unintelligible roar. Forrest looked into the agitated faces around him and for an instant wavered and nearly wept.

Morgan Lake, clad only in his drawers, pushed through the men to Forrest's side, his face grim. "These are not losers, General," he demanded, waving a hand toward the fort.

"They were the winners."

"This is no time for banter, Colonel," Forrest said. "Buckner has surrendered."

"The fort and his command!" Lake croaked. "We belong to neither! Did you surrender us?"

"God damn him, if he did!" a soldier shouted.

Forrest took no notice of the man's insubordination. It was like a slap waking him from a bad dream. He stepped up on a wood splitting log and looked down into the agitated, resentful faces. He had just made an instant decision and he prayed he was correct. "Keep your voices to a whisper. This cold air carries sounds for miles. Last night we departed quietly to gain a proper position on their flank. I now ask even more of you. Within two hours this camp must appear as though it was deserted days ago. We shall not be a part of this surrender. I am damn tired of being the tail that wags the dog. From now on we will be the first into battle with the most to take against the enemy. Let's get to it!"

"Damn right," they muttered. "The firstest with the mostest, that'll be us."

"But what of us?" Pedro silently asked Preacher.

Preacher thought it a fair question. His trust of Forrest was still on the borderline.

"General, the Whitworths don't leave without me, or the money to pay for them. Which is it?"

The question was rapped out so suddenly that Forrest had no time to think. He saw he was being forced into a corner and tried to bluster his way out. "Look, I don't have time to stand here and answer your damn fool questions. I am not responsible for the rifles, or you."

"The hell you're not! On your miserable, stinkin' promise I rode my tail off, nearly got killed and came back to find myself called a traitor. I've been used for the last time by the likes of you, Pillow and Floyd!"

The concentration of bitterness and defiance in the voice took the General unawares. This outburst could have a deeply unsettling effect on the already agitated men. It was no time for an apology, although he knew one was due. Nor could he praise Preacher for his calm in the counsel of war meetings, or for what had been reported to him of his shooting from the ramparts. To save all of his men, he had to be commanding.

He said curtly, "My quartermaster will see to your payment out of my private purse. You and your boy may ride with us to safety. Then, and only then, will I consider your insubordination!"

Preacher didn't flinch. He had spoken his piece and he held the upper hand.

"Sorry, General," Morgan Lake whispered, when Preacher had moved on. "He's still a damn good man."

"I did not say otherwise," he sighed. "Morgan, every man is afraid of something. Even you and me. But not that one. He has already walked into the Valley of the Shadow of Death and fears no evil. He is good, too good. The men will come to hate him because he is good. For one fleeting second today I felt a flash of tired helplessness, then I straightened my shoulders and set my jaw. Morgan, in this day of defeat, we suffered a single casualty—a horse shot out from beneath me. Time to go into our valley of death."

And, it was nearly that. A thrill of hope ran through the Union forces accustomed to defeat and retreat. Grant had his victory and wished no escapees. Patrols numbered twenty or thirty, instead of two or three. The cold front brought with it moisture, but even nature was against them. It wasn't warm enough to make it snow, so the driving moisture came down as sleet, as hard biting as buckshot pellets. The Union patrols shot Very gun after Very gun to spot troop movements from the fort. The rockets exploded five hundred feet up, but the sleet washed the red mushrooms out of the sky before they had time to form.

Still, they forced Forrest farther inland, rather than upstream. The rainy sleet turned the forest into a flooded backwater. The horses began slipping and sliding and balking.

Nate Forrest had a new mount. There was a tremendous crash of lightning and a tree at the edge of the forest exploded in flames. The mare began screaming and kicking in terror. There was no time for niceties. Forrest hit her a blow on the side of the head that numbed his hand and staggered the horse. She plowed into saddle deep icy water and balked. He started to lash her with a whip to get her to move when another horseman plowed in beside him. The horseman jumped into the water, which came to his chest, and took the mare by the bit. The horse danced nervously in place in the icy water. The man nuzzled the horse's head and soothed softly. His own horse forged through the water, as though showing the way. The mare reared and went with the man, fetlocks splashing as she strained against the mud and wind.

The sleet was so heavy Forrest could see only the outline of the man and his horse. Another lightning bolt revealed it was Preacher. He was washed with resentment and pride, all as one.

The point man splashed back to wave them off. Almost immediately after that Preacher hauled the gasping horse to a stop. The forest walled them in on both sides—the great trees shrieking and bending to the weight of the storm. The next lightning flash revealed two Union soldiers pulling their horses by the reins through the backwater. They were moving at an angle away from the column. Forrest signalled a silent wait. The hand signal was passed back along the line.

Then, luck turned against them. In front of the Union soldiers, a huge windfall blocked their way. There was no getting through it or around it. The soldiers turned and came directly towards them. When they were within forty feet, the rear soldier staggered and fell forward into the water. A muddied figure came out of the tangle of the underbrush, plunged his hand into the water, withdrew it and whip-lashed his arm forward again. The Bowie knife sliced into the back of the first soldier, as it had the second. His gurgle of death was covered by the wind.

Never one to waste a thing, Pedro took the reins of the Feds' horses and brought them back.

"Did you teach him that?" Forrest asked.

"No, sir," Preacher said, awed for the first time in a long while. "But I sure figure on having him teach me."

The windfall was also their problem. From the pack mules they brought forward a half dozen double-bladed axes. Officers and men waded into the tangle of wet wood and slashed at the broken branches. Here there was no rank or privilege. Forrest, Morgan Lake and Brent Barrett took their turns. In less than five minutes the massive tree was clean for a width of several horses. One by one they were brought to the barrier and forced over. The better trained horses made it from a standing jump. The mules had to be unloaded, whipped over and reloaded.

Throughout, General Forrest stood right by the tree to help and encourage each man and horse over the barrier.

Preacher stayed near at hand. To his surprise, he found that Forrest knew not only the name of every one of his men, but the names of their horses as well. The General's horse and Thor were the last over. The General's horse stood trembling and rolling its eyes in fear.

"Take Thor for awhile, sir. He'll let you mount if I tell him it is all right."

"Hardly," Forrest wheezed from near exhaustion. "I take no man's personal horse from him. I do kindly thank you for your help with Betsy, but she will be all right. It is only jealousy, my boy. Barney and Betsy were twin foals. She always resented it when I used Barney and not her stout back. Neither of us have had a chance to grieve his loss today. She resents that, too. Animals feel loss like human beings. Ride ahead, Preacher. Betsy and I need to have a family chat."

Here was yet another measure of the man that Preacher had to take under consideration.

Then, his concern became centered on Pedro. He found him shivering in his saddle, still caked from head to foot with mud. He wrapped blanket after blanket about Pedro's shoulders until he looked like a little Mexican man huddled under his serape.

Still, Preacher worried. Few had been close to him in life, and he had been close to few. The spunky kid reminded him of himself—forced to grow into manhood too soon.

Beyond the forest they came to a road. The horses were weakening rapidly now. Not even a whip could make them move faster. The point guards returned. It was only five miles to Faxon—two miles to the Faxon bridge—and a Confederate sentry post. Beyond the bridge they would be back among friends.

The storm abated, the sun rose, but did not bring with it warmth. Nate Forrest checked his map for Faxon. He cringed. They were six hours from Fort Donelson and had covered only twelve miles, less because they were still not at Faxon.

A mighty explosion mushroomed into the dawning sky. He knew at once that the bridge was out. Not only out, but the quiet creek now was raging white water from the storm. No power on earth could get an exhausted cavalry across that fury. For a moment Forrest felt beaten, helpless, but something stronger than his exhaustion drove him to the flooded riverbank. The stumps of the bridge supports were still visible.

"Ropes!" he bellowed. "Make a safety line from support to support."

"General, there's a train trestle a hundred yards upstream."

"Idiot suggestion," Captain Trent Clement screamed, his nerves at the shattering point. "Easier for a horse to swim than make him learn to walk railroad ties."

"Agreed," Forrest shouted, his chest heaving like a great bellows. "Leave me twenty men to swim the horses across. The men will cross on the trestle, but pulling up the rails behind them. I don't want Grant steaming down upon us on an iron horse."

Forrest stayed to command the twenty and noticed halfway through the operation that Preacher and Pedro were in the group.

"Why did you keep the boy with us?" Forrest called.

"He needed a bath, General."

"The water is warmer than the air," Pedro chuckled, swimming another horse across.

Nathan Bedford Forrest took a deep sobbing breath. Three more miles, he told himself. Just three more miles and they can all have rest and hot food.

It was not to be.

An hour later, after rejoining men to horse, the column halted in the center of a deserted village. At the end of the street stood a Confederate Lieutenant and six riflemen at the right and ready position.

"Hey, Reb! We ain't the enemy," sounded a call from the

ranks.

The young officer flushed. "Advance and name your unit."

"Forrest's raiders," a tired chorus of a hundred shouted.

The line of riflemen grew taut. The young officer hesitated.

Preacher drew alongside Forrest.

"Pardon, General," he said politely. "May I speak?"

"Yes?" he replied.

"I'm a gunslinger, for sure, who reads eyes. Those six have been told to shoot the man who says he commands this group. Look at their officer. Damn, he's almost too pretty to be a boy. Let me worm some truth out of him, if you will."

Forrest grunted. His regard for Preacher was on the slide again.

"Howdy," Preacher called, giving a special Eastern Tennessee twang to his voice. "Name's Preacher. Might you be having a name, Lieutenant, sir?"

James Ludlum Brice swelled a little at Preacher's use of a title and respect.

"James Ludlum Brice, attached to the Western Army of General A.S. Johnston. Now, instruct your men to drop their weapons and surrender."

"Why?" Preacher asked suddenly, before Forrest could react.

Brice laughed. Preacher studied every nuance in his face. The man was all blond, from hair to eyebrow to mustache; his eyes a pale blue; his lips a natural pink. Preacher sought for a word and came up with soft.

"A coward surrendered Fort Donelson with nearly twelve thousand men in uniform. Those men are now being marched to a prison camp in their winter underdraws and their uniforms used to make us think Yankees are Rebs. I said, drop your weapons, you damn Yankee spies!"

"Is that why you blew up the bridge?"

"Damn right! To stop you!"

"Boy, you are a damn fool!" Morgan Lake shouted.

Preacher gave Morgan a swift, significant look. They had never really worked in tandem before. They let their minds mesh. Morgan looked soberly at Preacher and then down to his holsters. He had watched Preacher's eyes roam the six riflemen and avoid the young officer. Morgan knew, as Preacher knew, that young Brice was too cowardly to pull his gun. The riflemen were their target.

"No one dares call me a fool!" Brice shouted. "Fire at will!"

Preacher took it as a command. He and Morgan were only four guns against six, but had the advantage of being on horseback and aiming down at the riflemen. And, as if they had communicated, they did not seek death, but an example.

With rapid chatter they got off a combined eight shots before the riflemen could think. The riflemen dropped their exploding and shattered weapons as though they had become live snakes.

Pedro and Brent Barrett charged off their horses like rockets, taking a stand in front of Lieutenant Brice.

"Game's over, Lieutenant," Barrett said. "We are who we say we are."

"Only guerrilla gunslingers shoot like that," Brice said angrily.

"Just thank God you are both on the same side. Normally, they shoot to kill."

"We're wasting valuable time," Forrest barked. "Where is your signal officer?"

"I'm afraid I'm everything," Brice said sheepishly. "We are only a rear guard patrol."

"Does that mean you have a telegraph or not?" Forrest asked flatly.

"Have," Brice gulped, and quickly added: "General, it's this way, at the train depot." He started to say more when a locomotive whistle cut through the air. "That would be the morning train from Murray, Kentucky."

"Idiot!" Forrest growled. "All of Kentucky is in the hands of the Feds. Morgan, get the men between the buildings. Lieutenant, get your men out of sight. Barrett, work your way to the depot and get ahold of General Johnston. Lookouts to the rooftops. I want to know who is on that train."

Everyone moved but James Ludlum Brice. He had been an

officer for only two months and the czar of Faxon for a month. He had been disgraced in front of his men and the towns-people. He held two men accountable for his disgrace. The one man had called himself Preacher. He would not forget the name or the man's shooting ability. Back home at Brice's Cross Roads, Mississippi, he was considered quite handy with his guns. He watched the man named Preacher and a young Mexican lad take their horses into the open doors of the livery. He turned to follow and quickly turned back.

The train ground to a screeching halt and blasted a warning signal with its whistle. He ran, instead, toward the end of the street and the road to the trestle. He began to wave and shout, having become friendly with the engineer and fireman. Then he stopped short. At his end of the trestle were a pile of iron rails. He cursed the guerrilla gang for doing this and not telling him. He started forward again when guards appeared on the roof of the first train car. They were armed, in Union blue, and opened fire at once.

The dirt began to splay up around him. He hit the ground and rolled backwards, the bullets inching closer. Shouts came from the sentries on the Faxon rooftops, but he figured he was a dead man who had walked into a foolish trap. He clawed, crablike, to get out of the Union rifle range. Then he heard a high, whining zing and hoofbeats. He heard two screams of pain from the train before he was grasped by the back of his belt buckle and hauled up to the back of a saddle. He didn't question. He just grabbed the rider about the waist as the horse sprung back towards town. The only sound was the quiet chugging of the idling locomotive, then, it's iron wheels made sparks as it spun into reverse.

In front of the livery he crawled down from Thor. It was bitter gall to say the words, but he was Southern born and bred. "Sir, I owe you my life. By Mississippi tradition, my family home is your home."

Preacher didn't have to say that General Forrest had given him a direct order to go save the fool, for Barrett was calling for an assembly.

It was another eye opener for Preacher. The Raiders, no matter their rank, were included in an assembly call.

"General Johnston has set up headuarters in Corinth, Mississippi. He's jubilant that we made an escape. He's amassing a force of 40,000 because he has news that the Yankees are going to come straight down the Tennessee River. We are not to engage them."

"Bullshit! General says we'se ta git there fustest with the mostest!"

"We are not to engage them," Barrett repeated emphatically. "Our guerrilla mission is far more important, and dangerous. We are to make sure that their supply lines are cut, thwarted and destroyed."

"What say you, General?"

Nate Forrest shrugged. "I'm hardly a military genius." He laughed. "Military history I leave to Morgan Lake. Still, these past weeks tell me we are not up against a fool. Grant will be as pugnacious as Hannibal crossing the Alps with elephants. An army is nothing without a supply line. I rather like the challenge."

"Then we are with you!" came a chorus.

"Could it have been otherwise," he said drily, then turned to Morgan Lake. "Colonel, as of this moment we have a new unit within this brigade. In the next few days, Sergeant J.D. Preacher will determine who are the best sharpshooters in this battalion. He, and he alone, will pick the ten finest."

"General," Morgan whispered. "We have twenty-four of the rifles, plus his own."

"I can count," Forrest hissed. "We are held at the stupid number of 100 horsemen. I will give him ten percent, but hardly a full quarter. The Virginia Command may have been correct, he is too good, too young, too arrogant. But, my needs are now. If Halleck is stuck with a General who drinks too heavily and disobeys orders, then I am one up on him."

"I beg your pardon?"

"I don't see Preacher constantly nipping on a bourbon bottle."

Neither was Grant. But rumors were rife out of St. Louis that he was drinking heavily. Ironically, the rumors gave Preacher the testing and training time that he needed. The rumors delighted Halleck and he removed Grant from command. The hero of the moment was vanquished and the war in the West stalled.

The next morning Brent Barrett rode into camp and found Nate Forrest. "Message from that Lieutenant Brice at Faxon, General. He's pulling out. The Feds are moving their supplies south by mule train."

"Let's break camp and ride."

They pounded leather for two hard days and saw no supply train. They headed southwest, reasoning that if Grant knew that Johnston was gathering troops at Corinth, Mississippi, then the Yankees and their supplies would be coming down the Big Sandy River valley.

On the fourth morning they saw a dust cloud on the horizon. There had been a rain the night before, so Forrest kept his Raiders to spring plowed fields and wet grassland. When they were close enough to spy, they were disappointed.

"From the battle standards they are only a part of Grant's army," Preacher said, looking through the telescopic sighting of his rifle.

"And no supply convoy," Forrest grunted.

Preacher had to smile. The man had kept one of the Whitworth telescopes, because it was stronger than his spy-glass. And, he had increased the number of sharpshooters under Preacher from ten to fifteen.

They watched from their hiding place for three hours. It was almost comical. It was a disorganized marching unit, made up mainly of green recruits from the reserve forces at Paducah. They were doing no scouting and had taken three rest stops in three hours. And in that three hours nothing else came over the horizon.

"What'll we do about them?" Barrett asked.

"Nothing," Morgan laughed. "At their rate of speed it will take them a week to get to Corinth Just foot soldiers and their mess wagons."

"Yes," Forrest mused. "No cavalry or cannon caissons. Curious. Preacher, when you were in Paducah, how many barges did the Feds have?"

"The Ohio was filled with them."

"I should have thought of that question sooner,

gentlemen. Brice said mule train, which would be needed to bring the wagons from the Tennessee River to Corinth. Map, please.''

In as direct a line as they could travel, they force marched southeast. Two miles above Savannah, Tennessee, they came across what was left of Brice's unit.

They were only three and carried Brice in a fireman's carry. His pretty, boyish face was no longer pretty. Numerous fists had pounded it into a black and blue swollen mask.

"Night patrol," he wheezed, "from Grant's advance force in Savannah. Thought we were part of your guerrilla force. They wanted no noise, so they strangled, knifed and beat with fists. They thought we three were dead. The rest are.''

Forrest clenched his teeth stubbornly. "Then Grant's supply train is already here?''

One soldier rubbed his throat and spoke. "No, sir. As I was being choked they laughed how no guerilla group would find it on its river route. Sounds to me like it ain't here yet, General.''

Forrest listened, but wanted the subject changed. "Brice, you need medical care. I have no corpsman or doctor. Are we near to where you might have friends?''

"Home," he sighed. "Brice's Cross Roads is about twenty miles south.''

"Bring them horses," he growled. "Lake, pick five men, all good shots, to see them safely home. We shall see to the supply train and then come back for our men. We will comb every bank and cove of the Tennessee until we find that supply train.''

Barrett looked on in helpless disapproval. The men were ready to drop from exhaustion and were saddle sore. But, he also knew they could hardly camp that close to Grant's army.

Still, Forrest was not inhuman. Once he had reached the river, he found a steep bluff with deep, wooded pockets on its surface. Here, he let them camp, but with no fires. They didn't mind. It was just nice to sit with nothing moving beneath them. They used their knives to open tins of salt pork and hard tack. They ate half, dozed off, then finished it off.

The picket-sentry duty fell to Preacher's Fifteen. He

divided them into groups of three. They didn't mind. It gave them an hour on and four hours to sleep.

It was the Ides of March. Spring was heavy upon the land. It was a balmy, peaceful night.

Chapter 12

THE SENTRY HAD quietly alerted Preacher. At once Preacher positioned his sharpshooters forward and held the rest to total silence.

They had been hoodwinked. They had not been able to find the supply train on the western side of the river, or on river barges, because it had been brought secretly down the eastern side of the Tennessee River, within enemy territory, where no one would think to look for it.

They came down out of the Highland Rim Hills at dawn in a long train of three hundred wagons pulled by six and eight-up mule teams. Two thousand cavalrymen rode beside the wagons and artillery carriers.

The heavily loaded wagons jolted and swayed as they serpentined on the river road between the bluffs. At one point, the road ran between a steep bluff and the river flatlands. Preacher looked to his right where the river grew wider, calmer, and several hundred pole barges waited on the opposite bank.

He had no time to consider the barges. He mentally judged the distance to the narrow turn on the opposite bluff, the portion of road he could not see, and the serpentine turns into the hills.

Forrest, Lake and Barrett came for a counsel of war.

Nate Forrest had considered the barges. "They are under guard by men in blue. I take them, therefore, to be Tennessee rivermen who may not be too happy with their lot. Preacher, how long can you stall that supply train?"

"As long as you wish, General."

"Give us fifteen to twenty minutes to get to the barges on

this side of the river," he said. "Colonel Barrett, have your special unit change into their Union uniforms. You will arrive first. When you get there, I want you to order the guards to take a break in that stand of woods. We will handle them silently. Take a pole barge across. We will follow as soon as the rivermen understand who we are and what we are about. Let's ride!"

Preacher spent the next fifteen minutes positioning each man, giving them a specific location to cover and setting Pedro to work on preparing every empty cartridge available.

Still Preacher waited until the train was fully out of the hills and committed to the river road and the narrow turn at the bluffs. Then he calmly trimmed the sights on his rifle and waited for Barrett to reach the opposite bank.

Preacher's men had been grumbling over what they thought was a foolish order, until they saw his tactic begin to work.

He let four wagons get through the narrow turn and onto the river flatlands. Then he aimed right between the lead mule's eyes. The mule stopped dead in his tracks. Then the mule in the companion hitch stopped dead. The teamster had heard nothing and began cracking his long whip over their heads. Finally the other four mules started balking over the smell of death.

Preacher raised his sight to the mule team in the narrow turning. Six shots and six mules fell. The turning was blocked. It was the signal for the other sharpshooters. Far to his left the riflemen concentrated on the wagons in the rear of the line. Their range was close to two miles and it took time before they had fully adjusted and started to fell the animals. Wagon after wagon began to block the road. Even at that distance they could hear the mounting "Yee-haws" of the teamsters and then their confusion as they realized their animals were mysteriously dead.

The guarding cavalry began to ride back and forth in total confusion and bewilderment. That was the signal for the shooters in the center. The round crowns of the officers' hats were centered in the cross hairs of the telescopic sights. The directing officers slumped and fell from their mounts. Still, not a shot had been heard. They scanned in every direction with spy-glasses. A regiment charged into the Highland Rim hills, only to come back shaking their heads. As they rode back, Preacher and his fifteen men dispatched them as casually as though they were firing into a herd of charging buffalo.

Preacher called a momentary halt. Pedro raced along the line with fresh ammunition, gathered up the spent cartridges and replaced malfunctioning rifles from their reserve of nine. It was a lull to allow Forrest to complete his work with the bargemen, regroup, and ride with his eighty-five into the very hills that the regiment had just departed.

As soon as the barges started poling back to their Chattanooga base, Preacher raised his hand, waited and dropped it.

There were twenty-seven cannon carriers scattered among the three hundred wagons. Preacher had learned in Missouri that each following wagon would be carrying cannon balls and black powder kegs. Fifteen sharpshooters concentrated on fifteen such wagons. Preacher zeroed in on a cavalry officer trying to bring order out of chaos. The blond officer screamed as the bullet ripped him from shoulder to thigh. Teamsters were thrown from their perches as their wagons began to explode from within.

"*Caramba*!" Pedro screeched, as the sky was streaked with billowing clouds and whistling rockets. Burning debris from the exploded wagons swooped down on the dry weathered canvas and internal supplies. All along the line, flames ate the wagons, living mules went into a panic, and men coughed in the smoke that wreathed that place of death.

Bugle after bugle began to sound the charge from the wooded hills and bounced off the bluffs. It was also a Nate Forrest trick. A dozen of his Raiders had been trained in every bugle call so they could sound like several regiments of cavalry.

The teamsters began running in mass back along the burning column and up the serpentine road. Several hundred of the leaderless cavalry heard the bugle charge and individually determined that it was retreat or death. Retreat meant riding down and over the several hundred teamsters. Their frantic, dodging figures were trampled to the ground by the mad dash of galloping, yelling horsemen.

Forrest brought the Raiders from the woods in a straight, charging line, as though they were the first wave of many to come. They drove to within point-blank range of the remaining cavalry, and only an occasional pistol shot fell among them as they neared the burning wagons. Black smoke poured across the bluffs and river flatland, and the crackle of flames and exploding cartridge crates was loud in the ears of Preacher's men.

Suddenly over the din was the high, frantic call of a Union retreat. They had come down the Tennessee River as brave, disciplined men, but now spun about like frightened sheep departing in any direction they could find. Preacher watched the brilliance of Forrest's cavalry training of his men. They broke into pairs, dividing the enemy and routing them. In this manner, one man could keep his eye on the enemy while the other shot their horses out from under them. Once on the ground, cavalrymen became disoriented. For a few seconds they were on wobbly legs and a sudden look-up made them dizzy. In a situation such as this, they just collapsed to the earth and awaited death, or the battle to pass them by.

"*Señor* Barrett!" Pedro screamed and pointed.

Brent Barrett had been separated from his partner. He did not see the black-mustachioed lieutenant who came out of the smoke on the gallop, his sword slashing. Nate Breed had seen him and charged. The shining shaft passed over Brent's shoulder and he turned to see the Union officer swing the sword back toward Forrest. It was too late. Forrest's horse plunged and screamed as the blade gashed the shoulder of the mount and Forrest was pitched to the earth. Brent and the officer spun their horses about to charge each other, but the Yankee raised his blade for the final cut at a real prize—a Reb General. Then his contorted face flattened, and the sword dropped from his relaxed grip as he died. Brent Barrett and Nate Forrest didn't have to ask why they had not heard the reason for his death. Nate rose, pushed the dead man from his saddle and mounted. The horse did not know the difference between blue and gray.

"It's nice to have two extra eyes in this business," he muttered.

The rout was near complete. They rode slowly along the line of silent, shattered wagons. They were blazing fiercely now.

Oddly, halfway down the column, a wagon lay crazily tilted on its side with its shaft twisted and its four mules peacefully standing. Relaxed in death lay a Colonel, half in and half out of the tail gate. The interior of this wagon had been a field office for him.

Barrett climbed down and reached around the man to take the dispatch case from the fallen table. He found the latest document and handed it to General Forrest.

Forrest opened the dispatch and read it slowly while Barrett waited. "He was Stanley Fischer," he said. "Quartermaster for Grant."

"Why send such a top-ranking man in the quartermaster corps?"

Forrest read his orders:

"You will proceed in my rear with three hundred baggage, cannon, supply and ammunition wagons. General Anson Speller will escort you with the 32nd and 38th Cavalry. You will avoid battle, if possible, and meet a barge convoy below Peter's Landing between 15-17 March. I shall, by then, be head-quartered at Savannah, Tennessee. Johnston is below me some thirty miles. Between us on the Tennessee, is Pittsburg Landing. Our informant at Brice's Cross Roads advises this is an excellent supply depot. When Buell joins me, we will expand your supply line to Chattanooga.

Your servant
U.S. Grant"

"Simple and direct," Barrett said.

"Except Johnston and Beauregard didn't think Grant would fully move till late March."

Barrett laughed. "With no supplies, it might take that long."

Forrest scowled. "I don't like that bit about an informant

at Brice's Cross Roads. That's where we sent men with Brice. It's where I thought we might rest for a few days. Who is our best man to send ahead and start smelling around?"

Barrett laughed again. "Need I mention a name?"

"I was afraid you were going to say that. Signal across my congratulations and thanks for your life. Tell Preacher to move his men south to Brice's Cross Roads. You and Morgan will join him with the others. I'll head direct to Corinth."

"What do we tell Preacher about this informant?"

"Nothing, until I get back. Let him get to know the people naturally. Pedro will like it there. Merriweather Brice came up from Mexico in 1806. He brought with him Mexican cotton seeds and workers. Many are now third generation."

"It's positively uncanny." Betty Brice paused on the top step of the verandah and gazed over the silent Raiders with a shiver.

"The silence—yes," Preacher answered slowly. "They needed this rest."

"It's been a week and all they do is sleep and eat and sleep again."

"If we believe General Forrest, we may not get much sleep soon."

"Nonsense! All this feverish talk of violence so near—"

"You saw what they did to your son, James."

She started to tell Preacher a truth and changed the subject. "Which is why Grandfather Brice allowed the Raiders to camp right here and not off in a distant pasture. As an avowed Secessionist, he feels nothing is too good for the cause."

"And you don't believe that?" Preacher asked seriously.

She focused her sparkling brown eyes on him. He had been like a breath of fresh air coming into their world. At thirty she still had a fair young face, a firm body and strong-willed mind. She refused to wear widow's weeds, even though it put her in disfavor with Merriweather Brice.

"J.D., I was born and raised in Springfield, Illinois. As a girl, I got to know Mr. Lincoln and don't consider him a war-monger."

Preacher's slender figure stiffened. She had nearly laughed

when told there was a Union informant at Brice's Cross Roads. This was a peaceful world that seemed set apart. The little community reminded him of Bradburn Hill. Hard, industrious people who raised their special cotton for the reselling of the seed, rather than the bolls. The overseers, house staff and many of the small farmers were Mexican. They were neither Abolitionists nor Secessionists. Here was the first hint that someone might have a northern sympathy and he did not want to believe it of Betty Brice.

"Grant was aware of the supply train destruction nearly as quickly as Johnston in Corinth," Forrest told Preacher later.

"No one has arrived or departed here, but you," Preacher said musingly. "We've quietly watched everyone."

"Still, someone here is not a true Southerner."

On that point Preacher could agree, but he was not about to mention Betty Brice.

"Regardless, Grant is being resupplied by every means possible."

"Why didn't we attack when he was weak?" Morgan dryly observed.

"Johnston has been sitting on his ass waiting for his own destruction."

"And I haven't the slightest doubt on that point," Barrett said with quick emphasis.

"Anyhow," Forrest said smilingly, "General Beauregard and I have convinced him that our Rebel fortunes might be regained by a signal victory. Grant is still the target, because he is well forward of his base, is still unsupported by a supply line and has divided his forces. We shall move out at dawn on April 1st, gentlemen."

"April Fool's Day," Preacher chuckled. "What if we are fooled and there is an informant in this area?"

Forrest's lips slightly curved. "Then we shall one day be back for vengeance!"

Nothing was said, but the preparations over the next few days spoke for themselves. The Raiders were no longer sleepy. They cleaned their weapons, filled cartridges, saddle-soaped everything to soft leather form. They sang and frolicked. It was time to get back to the serious business of war.

But one was faced with the serious business of living.

A figure came into Preacher's tent before midnight, squatted by his cot, pale and determined to tell the truth. In halting English, Pedro told his account of the battle and the panic in which it had left him. Then, to his dismay, he told Preacher how surprised he had been to find people of his own tongue in this place.

"I'm sorry. I would like to stay with my good friend—but—but it's a pity to kill those you do not hate."

"What are you going to do?"

"I am going back to Mexico, and see if I am a man." He paused and scowled. "It is over a girl, and my curiosity's aroused. I cannot gain her unless I prove myself."

"Rubbish," Preacher cried. "You've proven yourself many times over. You're a trained rifleman. We need you here."

"Much thanks, *Señor*. My mind's made up. I begin my walk tonight."

Preacher laid a hand on Pedro's shoulder. "I shall miss you. What of this girl? Did you make love to her and now run in fear?"

Pedro flushed and shook his head. "Oh, how I wanted to be like you in the hold of the boat, but she would not allow. She loves me and will wait to be my wife."

"Don't wait," Preacher groaned. "If you wish her for your bride, take her with you, now. This war has no tomorrows."

"When you need me, you know my town in Mexico."

Pedro secured horses. The girl and her family were willing. The shadows of night gave them a chance to escape.

"Is he not your turncoat?" Merriweather Brice sternly demanded.

"How did you know we thought there was a turncoat?" Morgan Lake asked, perplexed.

"We are a small community. That rumor has been on my ear since your arrival. I said hog-wash!"

"Then the less said about it, the better. Let's hush it up."

The eighty-five year old man gave him a toothless grin. "Fine! I've already lost one son to this war, am stuck with a worthless Yankee daughter-in-law, and a grandson who can only get his damn face smashed in. Put the blame on the Mex and we'll drop it."

"But, you are the one who brought the Mexicans here in the first place."

"Don't mean I ever trusted them," he answered, with a touch of scorn. "How far do you trust a black man? I've felt the same, but they've now stuck a dagger in my back."

"Bullshit! He was one of ours and ran off with one of your young girls. That's all that has you upset. Was she good at picking cotton in the field?"

"We don't pick cotton," he scathed. "We take the seeds while they are subtle, before they crack open and dry." He blinked and his mind wandered. "Deserted, that's all they have done. Deserted this old man."

Betty Brice waved Morgan Lake away. She took Merri-weather Brice back into his Spanish style *hacienda* and turned him over to a servant. She felt a moment of desperation. The words between her father-in-law and the attractive Colonel were banal. She was now fighting for the life of her husband.

She went to the study and wrote a note to J.D. Preacher. She read it over and it seemed foolishly cold and formal. She tore it up and wrote a simpler one. It was flippant and a little presumptuous. She destroyed that and decided on a single line: "Can I see you a few minutes before we sit for our last supper?"

She sent it by her Mexican maid and began to hurriedly dress, her mind in a whirl of nervous excitement. Her vanity was such that she never even paused to ask whether her answer would be a yes. She was sure of it.

Her excitement lay in a thrilling discovery. Lawrence Brice had squired her away from Illinois with his dapper charm and her desire to escape spinsterhood. A honeymoon convinced her that Larry Brice wanted more than her long protected virginity. She was accepted at Brice's Cross Roads as a leper to be pitied and scorned. Betty Harmon Brice scorned scorn. Her expert brain was something Southern ladies were not expected to use. Larry Brice wanted her brilliance. She loved him for it. Now, she had an opportunity to serve him well.

And when at last he came, she would not disgrace herself by rushing downstairs. She waited for five minutes and then had him brought to her private chambers.

She led him to a window seat and she flushed with the

sudden realization that he had been holding her hand since
the moment he arrived. She drew it away with a quick,
nervous movement, and sat down abruptly.

"Am I in a position to ask a favor?" she asked with an
attempt at conventional tones.

"Depends upon the favor."

She hesitated and sighed. It was not lost on Preacher that
she was wearing a very low cut dress that molded her body in
a very exciting and suggestive manner. He had dreamed of
her in every possible sexual way, but this was hardly the
moment.

"I wish for you to take James with you to battle," she said
at last.

"Take James," he repeated mechanically.

"Yes. He is only my step-son, you know. Even though he
hates me, because of his father, I promised to speak on his
behalf."

"Is that your late husband?"

The room was very still. Betty turned her eyes toward the
oil painting over the fireplace. She nodded.

"Where have I seen that face before?"

"You see it every day when you look at James." Her voice
had a faraway sound as if she were talking to herself. "It is the
only thing that they have in common, their blond good
looks. Well?"

Again a silence fell between them. He looked steadily into
her brown eyes that were burning now with a strange
intensity. He knew that all he had to do was just look at the
bed and she would consent to win the favor. As enticing as it
seemed, he resented her motive. He had learned from experts
how a woman could use her sexual favors to gain her desires.
Had this scene taken place earlier, during his stay, he would
have been the one using sexual favors to learn a few truths.
Now, it was too late.

"I'm afraid I don't have that authority, Miss Betty."

She sprang to her feet trembling from head to foot.

"You must keep him under a close watch. I am frightened,
Preacher. He will kill me, but you are the only man I can
trust. It was not Yankees who beat on him, but some of his
own men when they found out that he and two of his men

were traitors. He has lied to you at every turn."

"Everyone has been watched, including James. How in the hell has he been getting messages to Savannah?"

"You watched everyone coming and going from the west and not the east. Our farm carts made daily trips to our docks on the lake and into the Tennessee. Savannah is only twenty miles downriver."

"But who? It's only been the Mexicans on those wagons."

"Because you thought he was spending most of his time in his room recovering. We use a great deal of hazel nuts as a brown dye. A temporary solution can turn blond hair brown, until it is washed out with lye soap."

"Tell James we ride within the hour, not tomorrow."

He walked from the room, his jaw set. He knew his decision would not set well with Nate Forrest, but he was prepared to take that heat. The door had scarcely closed when the trembling figure crumpled on the window seat in a flood of sighing relief. She had done it without having to bed the lad.

Then, his words brought her alert. She pulled the bell cord for her maid and went to the closet. She was down to her chemise by the time the maid came to take her message to James.

"And I find I am very tired. Tell Grandfather Brice that I am going directly to bed and will not be down for dinner."

Once alone, she put on a peasant skirt, blouse, covered her head with a shawl and pushed on the back wall of her closet. It opened onto a narrow, interior stairway. Larry Brice needed to know that Forrest's Raiders were leaving within the hour and not on the morrow.

Nate Forrest was wary of Preacher's report, but thought it best to keep James Ludlum Brice under a watchful eye. Morgan Lake thought the report of the disguise had some merit, because of Merriweather Brice's belief that the traitor was a Mexican. Still, he felt young Brice too arrogant and stupid to be such a successful spy.

They began to wonder if any spy report would have any meaning and purpose.

"It would seem, gentlemen," Forrest said sourly, "we have been brought to Cornith early because of our growing reputation over the supply train. Our Confederate Commander is absolutely sure that he can throw the flower of Grant's magnificent army across the river at Pittsburg Landing. Still, he is making a demand. He wants our sharp-shooter outfit assigned to one of his infantry units.''

Preacher groaned. He was being sold out again. James Brice was sticking to him like glue, which was an added insult. The only time he could be alone was when Nature called. Even then, he could not be alone.

''I thought your bladder would never fill,'' Nate Forrest said from the shadow of the trees. ''Keep peeing, I don't want Brice to know I am here. Johnston didn't ask for you, Preacher. That was my idea to help smoke out Brice. Your fifteen will ride independent. The rest of the Raiders need to vanish, to learn where Grant has his six divisions. Let Brice see all he wants to see and then vanish with his report. We know where to find him, when we want to find him.'' He chuckled. ''His report will be too late. We are prepared to crush the blue army like a robin egg shell.''

It was well planned, but in war the unexpected often happens.

The unexpected turned up as confusion, which caused delay. The rotation of march had been changed so many times to confuse enemies spies, that there was no movement. It took Johnston until April 3 to put his 40,000-man army on the road for Pittsburg Landing.

Preacher kept his fifteen, plus Brice, separate and composed.

''This is a disgrace,'' James Brice fumed. ''That is even more disorganized than Grant's movement south.''

''How?'' Preacher shrugged.

''Are you blind? The carefree, whooping, straggling undisciplined men makes the Yankees look like a professional army.''

Preacher grinned. Brice could not have seen the Yankees march south and still have wired them from Faxon post.''

Still, his frustration was also mounting. The line of march was taking so long that the day of battle was postponed from April 4 to the 5th and then quietly to the 6th.

James Ludlum Brice disappeared on the evening of April

5th. It was discovered after Preacher's fifteen had ridden far afield to scout the Union regiments in the Shiloh-Pittsburg force. The Union troops were so green that they were doing no scouting and had no outpost duty sentries. It amazed Preacher, because Johnston's noisy army was starting to bivouac just two miles away without being detected. Even if Brice got the ten miles north to Savannah, Grant would be able to do little before dawn. He knew it was time to rejoin Forrest's Raiders.

He was not aware that James Brice had met with an accident which caused his disappearance.

Looking down upon the white Union tents, in gravestone order around the silent Shiloh Church, Brice saw a familiar figure enter one of the tents. He left the fifteen with a feeling of dread, but with family fury. He was just approaching the tent after a successful stroll through the enemy camp wearing the uniform of a Confederate lieutenant. A rude and unsympathetic guard arrested him. James was greatly grieved at his unkind remarks.

"Lordy, man, you ought not to say things like that to me! I am not a spy!"

"The hell you're not. I can tell a Reb uniform when I see one."

"Forget the uniform. I saw my father enter that tent and I damn sure want to have a confab with him!"

"Ain't nobody in that tent with the Colonel except a dirty old Mexican. Now, off the horse. My Captain will be interested to learn why you are in these parts."

Preacher didn't have time to worry about James Brice. He was in on a counsel of war—if there was going to be a war.

"Hard to believe," General Forrest mused, "but their defenses are laid out in a very sloppy manner. Between that church and Pittsburgh Landing, two miles to the northeast, are five divisions. A sixth division is five miles north at Crump's Landing. Then another five miles to Savannah and Grant's main force. To divide his army like that means a death trap."

"For us," General Beauregard fumed. "The enemy cannot help but be forewarned because of our stupid delays. I know I proposed this attack, but I now feel it should be called off.''

"I disagree," Genral Johnston snorted. "I would fight them if they were a million. What say you, General Forrest?"

Forrest turned his keen blue eyes on the grey-haired General. "Contrary to all rules of military science, there is a way, sir. The front and left are strong, but an early morning attack will catch them off guard. I can swing my Raiders in a quick movement to the rear while you attack the front. The encampment around the church and beyond is under General William Tecumseh Sherman. He'll think it's a full retreat of the cavalry. Out of sight, we'll turn, cut him off from getting help from Wallace or Grant, and smash into his rear before sundown.''

Johnston quickly approved the amazing plan of the Raider commander, though it involved the necessity of a very bloody infantry battle.

Johnston might have breathed easier had he been in the tent of General Sherman.

"Really, Brice," Sherman said drily, "I have to question your word. You say a cavalry unit has come into the area from your home town. We capture your son, a member of that unit, and he claims only to be a part of a scouting patrol.''

The only bitterness Larry Brice held in his heart was toward his son. It was the wrong moment in time to play hero. He had worked too hard to save his little world from a senile father and the ravages of war. He could not let his son ruin his chances of survival.

"Damn it all," Larry Brice roared, "the boy lies! He was caught and I demand a firing squad in the morning."

Sherman looked disgusted. "He is your son."

"Caught as a spy to make my reports look foolish."

Sherman didn't like spies of any ilk. He waved the man away. In the morning he would put the man to the test by preparing his son for the firing squad. Then he sent a message to Grant that he anticipated no Rebel attack.

The next morning was a Sunday. It was five o'clock in the morning when Johnston's swift, silent marchers began to draw near to the unsuspecting Union forces encamped around the Shiloh Church. The artillery carriers had been moving forward throughout the night. The artillery horses were cropping the tender dew-laden grass with eagerness.

Preacher had led the Raiders back to his little lookout ridge on whose further hillside was the church near the banks of the Tennessee. The boys in blue were awakening for the day, their camp fires curling through the young green leaves for the start of their breakfast. The sun was coming up bright and hot. The Union division was unsuspecting. It was nearly six o'clock before Johnston's men had all slipped silently into position behind the dense woods on the little slope. In two long grim battle lines, one behind the other, with columns in support, his horse artillery with their big guns were ready.

The morning was so clear, and they were so near, that the telescopes were not needed. Then Preacher did raise the piece to his eye and his heart sank with deep pity. James Ludlum Brice was being marched to a little clearing where a firing squad awaited. Behind him marched a Mexican. Preacher focused on the face. He saw the deception at once. It had not been James Brice who had used the Mexican disguise, but the man from the portrait. Then another memory flashed back. The man in the portrait had been the main mule-skinner on the wagon train they had ambushed. But Preacher was helpless. To try and save James Brice would forewarn the attack.

Far to the left came a report of shots. A startled flock of quail swept from the woods and down to the encampment. Two Yankee patrol guards came running into camp announcing they had run into Rebel pickets. Sherman grew nervous. Brice was not batting an eye over the pending death of his son, and enemy pickets that close could mean an attack.

"Form the regiments in front of the tents," he commanded.

"But, it is Sunday, sir."

"War does not have a day of rest!" he boomed.

His voice echoed into the woods. Johnston's complete surprise was being taken away from him, but perhaps not momentum. He signalled the artillery. The hollow baying of the cannon did come as a surprise. The first regiments in sight were blown into atoms and driven back as chaff before a whirlwind. Behind them the regiments turned to see the

Confederates approaching in two long lines of butternut. The men leaped to their guns and fought desperately to stay the rushing torrent.

Ironically, the firing squad went about their business unperturbed. A white cloth was bound over James Brice's eyes. The sergeant dealt out the specially prepared round of cattridges—all blanks save one, so that no soldier might know who did the murder.

In low tones, Preacher ordered six of his sharpshooters to fire straight at the heart of the firing squad members. He sighted in on the sergeant. Just as the Whitworths flashed, Forrest gave the signal for the Raiders to ride. Preacher had a second to see the men crumple to the soft young grass and Brice race towards his son. Preacher moved his sights to the man, in case he personally tried to kill his son. To his surprise, Brice yanked off the blindfold and pulled James toward two waiting horses. They were going to make their escape from the battlefield. Preacher was pleased. He wanted Brice alive to meet him face to face, one on one.

Chapter 13

THE NEXT TWO hours were almost a blur in Preacher's mind. The Raiders smashed into Sherman's left flank and broke them. Johnston's boys in butternut swarmed into the camp. The Union regiments began to flee the field.

"Fall back and save yourselves," a Colonel called, before being the first to dash to the rear.

General Forrest had not counted on this. The Yankees were to think that he was in retreat, but the Raiders rode right into chaos. Without support, they could only attack.

Forrest snatched his hat off and waved for the charge. Battle ready, they crushed, crumpled and rolled through the green Yankee troops. The regiment was cut to pieces, horses, mules, cattle, guns, were in a tangled mass of blood and death.

One, two and then a third horse was shot from beneath Nathan Bedford Forrest. Each time he would mount a new one and dash about directing his men, whose number was also dwindling rapidly.

Beyond them was a ragged gap of a mile without a man, left bare by a division which had fallen back through a peach orchard to a sunken road about two feet deep and were taking picket positions in the ready-made trench.

"Barrett," Forrest shouted. "Get your men through that gap and attend to your primary mission! Preacher, prepare all guns!"

Preacher had not only been preparing all his guns, but snatching them up off the battlefield and giving them to other Raiders.

The sturdy horsemen plowed their way through the receding blue waves of panic-stricken men and dashed toward the peach orchard.

Benjamin Prentiss now had his men under control in the sunken road. Because of the manner in which the road bent around, he could control a Rebel attack from Shiloh and also protect the rear of the Union retreat until the leaders could straighten out the battle lines.

The fighting now became a battle. It was no longer a rout.

Three times Forrest charged with his gallant Raiders. Three times they were driven back from almost certain death.

"It's a damn hornet's nest," Preacher fumed. "They are so concealed that not even the Whitworths can get at them."

The morning stretched on. Forrest got his men into a grove of trees and took stock. He had lost forty-two men, eight of them sharpshooters. He now believed Preacher. The Whitworth was just another rifle in the hands of an inexperienced man. He vowed, if they lived through this blood-bath, that every Raider would learn how to use the piece.

Barret returned, his mission a success. His Union dressed Raiders had been able to get to the Crump's Landing road before General Lew Wallace's division arrived. They sent them on the road to Grand Junction and away from Shiloh.

Morgan Lake returned from reporting to General Johnston in a blind fury.

"His damn men stopped fighting once they got into the tent streets and started looting and eating the Yanks' breakfast. Beauregard is pinned down by McClernand's cannons and has plugged up Sherman's collapsing left. Johnston is preparing to attack that road entrenchment. He is so sure of victory that we are to stay where we are and stop the retreating entrenchment soldiers from retreating."

Sixty cannon brought into the peach orchard thundered at the hornet's nest. The butternut lines flowed against Prentiss' placement. Time after time the high fierce cry of the Rebel yell was shouted down by the victorious Northerners, leaving only the screams of stricken horses and the wail of dying men. On the eleventh charge, General Johnston swung his own division into line and ordered them to follow him at bayonet ready. He fell at the head of his men.

"We are missing our opportunity for victory because of that one position," Forrest growled. He saw that Thor was riderless and his heart nearly sank. "What has happened to Preacher?"

Morgan Lake pointed far to their right and to the next grove.

Preacher had been crawling undetected through the tall grass and had started to climb a tree. He was spotted at once. Four horsemen charged up out of the sunken road. Before Preacher could raise his Whitworth a shell exploded squarely between the four, hurling them into the air. Their dying cries rang pitifully through the smoke-wreathed woods. One horse neighed a long, quivering, soul-piercing shriek of agony and Preacher drew his revolver and killed him. The hell of the battle was not so hot that the Yankees had lost their sense of humane treatment for the animals. From the entrenchment, Preacher was cheered.

It gave him time to climb the tree. The cheers in the trench turned to anguish.

Preacher fought for an hour from the top of the tree. Twice the bullets striking the bark knocked pieces into his eyes. He was sure at least a hundred minie balls struck the tree trunk but didn't pierce it. Still Prentiss' gunners kept falling one by one, falling ominously at the crack of a single gun in the woods.

Forrest would wait no longer. Preacher had this end of the road pinned down. He took the Raiders into battle double-quick. The Yankees turned and hurried down the road. Beauregard, now in command, saw them coming and ordered another attack. The men in grey charged and drove the Yankees a hundred feet before Prentiss rallied his men and pushed the Rebs back with frightful loss on both sides.

But from his rear came the Raiders.

As the Raiders rushed by Preacher's tree at double quick, Preacher spotted a panic-stricken officer crouching in terror behind a rock. His revolver was shaking, but he could still kill several Raiders before they would spot him. Preacher aimed and the Whitworth only clicked. He cursed himself for having lost his reloading count. By the time he was reloaded, he heard the pistol's sharp bark. He heard the ugly smacking sound of lead striking flesh. He knew that sickening sound too well.

Brent Barrett fell, dangerously wounded, and lay fifty feet beyond Preacher's tree. Preacher coolly leaped from the tree, walked out in a hail of lead, picked up his friend and carried him safely into the grove.

"Funny," Brent muttered. "It don't hurt."

It had not been the officer's bullet. A flying piece of shrapnel had torn a hole in his back and cut into his spinal chord.

The night was drawing her merciful veil over the scene at last. At 5:30 pm Prentiss surrendered. Moments later rain fell in torrents, as though God could no longer hold back his tears.

With nightfall, Lew Wallace arrived, unsure how he had taken the wrong road. Moments later General Buell's advance guard reached Grant from the northeast.

The counsel of war was held in Sherman's captured tent at Shiloh. What a difference twenty-four hours had made. The night before General Beauregard had been recommending that the battle be called off.

"Gentlemen, I have informed Richmond of our great victory this day. Tomorrow, we shall. . . ."

His words trailed off into silence. He couldn't bring himself to think of what it might bring.

At dawn, with the fresh divisions arrived on the field, Grant ordered a surprise attack. The overcast skies made the dawn as still as night. The long lines of blazing muskets in the gloom looked like a prairie fire out of control. In eager anticipation of a quick victory, the Union commanders moved too many men too quickly. A wall of blue was moved forward to capture the lost ground, but at a frightful loss. Later, no man wanted to consider how many Northerners were shot down by their own comrades in the confusion of the mad attack orders, or from the use of the gunboats Tyler and Lexington which had been moved down from Savannah during the night. Their cannon were to fire down the length of the Confederate line, but were never sure when their own troops had captured and gone beyond that line.

The leaden sky held down the smoke until it was near impossible to see.

Near noon the sun briefly broke through. Time enough for each side to see that Shiloh had been two of the bloodiest days in the Civil War. The sun vanished and so did the Confederates. Beauregard's army was exhausted and outnumbered. Wreathed in smoke, he ordered a retreat to Corinth, leaving 10,700 dead behind.

"Grant let them go," Buell fumed, when General Henry Halleck arrived that evening at Pittsburg Landing.

"Nonsense," Sherman countered, "we had quite enough of their society for two whole days, and were only glad to be rid of them on any terms."

Buell, fresh to the battle, was adament. "General Halleck, I demand this command and authority to pursue!"

Halleck loved it. It gave him an opportunity to fire Grant once again, but he hated Don Carlos Buell more than Grant.

"No, I am taking personal command and will lead the pursuit. But, not until I have had a good night's sleep."

He would actually have many nights of good sleep. It took him 31 days to march the 20 miles to Corinth, only to find the town evacuated. He was being very cautious. The Northern press were aghast at the loss of 13,700 Yankee soldiers sacrificed by the heartless butchers of the Western Command.

Nathan Bedford Forrest took his shattered Raiders back to Brice's Cross Roads. Their wounded bodies and the agony on their stark faces told the hideous story of their ordeal more plainly than words. This time their welcome was wary.

Preacher's main concern was for Brent Barrett. They had brought him back by stretcher, strapped between two horses. The surgeon in Corinth had taken a single look and turned to the wounded whose lives he could save.

Betty Brice was uncivil. "You will bring death down upon us all."

Preacher was stunned. Her opening salvo never once

questioned the whereabouts of her step-son. Then his heart turned cold. Never once had she spoken of her husband in the past tense. They were among enemies as surely as being back at Shiloh.

But, Merriweather Brice proved to be less than senile. His Mexican workers had a doctor among them. The old Mexican was frightened, but did as Merriweather commanded.

Preacher held Brent's hand while the knife cut through the soft flesh and found the imbedded piece of shrapnel. The grip of the slim fingers tightened, but Brent gave no cry. His breath came in quick gasps and he was about to faint.

"Damn it! I felt that pain."

The doctor met Preacher's eyes. They were hopeless. Preacher knew then that Brent had felt nothing, would never again feel a thing from his chest down.

Preacher became Brent's constant nurse. His one desire was to get Brent well enough to move home to Tennessee.

The report from Shiloh drifted slowly, ominously, appallingly, over the small community. With the Union so close, the community greatly feared harboring Confederates.

Betty Brice was quick to answer the message that her husband and step-son were at Pickwick Lake. The long days with no word of them had paralyzed her senses.

Her father-in-law was at breakfast alone.

"I must get to the caves and the lake. They are safe and are being joined by friends. They will help us rid ourselves of our unwelcome guests."

The old man suddenly rose with a fierce light flashing in his eyes. "Oh, the miserable blunderer I sired. His whole attitude in this war is loathsome to me. We cannot play both sides and come out the winner."

"Don't be inconsistent," she barked. "You blamed him at first for trifling with the war, then supported him when you saw the money he could make for the family as an arms dealer. Now you blame him because the war has come too near to your precious home."

He shook his grey head in protest. "It was easy to fool our people, because they had no reason to distrust our word. Even the simple mind of James could be twisted. These cavalrymen are not easily twisted."

"Wait," she soothed, "for your brilliant son has Bill Quantrill with him at the lake."

"But, he is a Rebel guerrilla leader!"

She smirked. "He is a leader of deserters and desperadoes who like money. We don't mind paying for survival, do we?"

Preacher had been wary of Betty Brice since his return, but that morning paid little attention to her departure. He was busy getting Brent onto a mattress in a flat-bed wagon. Brent and three of the other wounded Raiders were to be taken to the Tennessee for a boat trip to Chattanooga and then home.

A hour later she returned, cold, wordless and pale. A strange ominous stillness settled for a moment, then all hell broke loose.

A great shout swept from all directions. Quantrill's Raiders, purposely in Confederate grey, swept into view, eager for the fray. They rapidly deployed to the right and left. The left group rode down on the tired and exposed Raiders with a wild shout, their eyes set for murder. The right group fired into the Mexican compound houses. Then, they turned toward their main mission objective.

With a single mighty impulse, that group of guerrilla riders surged toward the *hacienda* doors and through them. A sound of smashing glass, screaming horses and Rebel yells. Merriweather Brice rushed from his home holding money above his head.

"You are here to help me, men—here is your money!"

The guerrilla band tore the money from his grasp and let the hooves of their horses paw him to pulp.

The Raiders couldn't help the old man. The attack had been well planned, as if that force had prior knowledge as to their strength and tent placement. They were lucky to get off a single shot in that first surge. Those still inside the *hacienda* smashed the furniture into kindling wood, piled it in the middle of the main rooms and set fire to it. Seeing this, the Mexican workers began to leave. Then they were chased and beaten and the young women run down and raped.

"Why?" they shouted.

The answer was always the same, in Spanish and English. "We are Forrest's Raiders. The Yankees must know we have been here."

It was believed, because the Mexican workers saw only the grey uniforms they had been used to seeing.

In their panic they did not see that the half a hundred Raiders were regrouping and fighting back. Fighting back to the point of starting to win. The Quantrill deserters and desperadoes had no stomach for the battle line. They preferred the sudden swoop attack and quick getaway. This was proving not to their liking, no matter the amount of money offered. They began to vanish back into the woods as the Raiders' aim became more deadly.

Preacher had watched, getting in his shots, but troubled by the fire in the main *hacienda*. It was now an inferno. No one could live through that.

Over and over again he repeated the anger in his mind. "She isn't worth a moment's thought!"

Then he saw the doors of the stable open and a figure beckon to two approaching riders. The riders were an old Mexican and James Brice. He dropped the Whitworth and began to dodge hot lead. The struggle between good and evil had just taken a strong twist.

The Raiders were forcing back the double numbered Quantrill men. Preacher was able to get to the back of the stable and through a door. He crept forward. The argument was loud in his ears.

"My father!" Larry Brice screamed. "Why did you let him be trampled to death?"

"It had to be," she said coldly and impersonably. "I feared he would warn them before I could get back to start the attack."

"I didn't order his death," he wailed.

"But would have allowed the death of James," she snapped.

"Nonsense," he snorted, "I had that under control."

James Brice laughed derisively. "Control? I'd be dead if there had not been that Yankee attack. Shit, I've played the fool for a pittance—and nearly got shot. I still may be shot as a traitor."

"James," Lawrence Brice growled, "you have done well in my eyes. You diverted the enemy, but they proved too smart. Believe me, I never would have let you be shot by a firing squad."

"What of grandfather?" James insisted.

"Damn good question," Preacher growled, stepping into the center of the stable. "Who did kill him? I liked that old man. He was stability, you are all greed. But I am a reasonable man, and am willing to let you speak."

"Reasonable," Betty grumbled. "He was the greed behind all of our thoughts."

Preacher smiled. "Because he is dead and can't defend his motives."

He had just stirred their emotions into a jam. They had been blaming each other and could now, in an odd way, place their blame on him.

"Except," Lawrence Brice grinned, triumphantly, "you will never live to question his motives, wants or last thoughts."

His grin had alerted Preacher to watch him carefully. Betty and James Brice were unarmed. Larry Brice, under his loose fitting Mexican shirt, wore a brace of pistols. The low hanging shirt hit the holster hilts. Preacher, after months of war, went back to his basics. He watched Brice's eyes.

"Are you aware, young man, that I have killed no less than eight men in duel matches?" Brice sneered.

Preacher calmed. "They say I've killed a man for every year of my life. Don't ask my age. If this is a callout, the call is yours."

Brice laughed, a little nervously. "We are at war. Soldiers, so to speak. I hear you are quite an expert with the rifle and kill men at will."

"That's war," Preacher grinned, then sobered. "I don't like this war. I don't like cheats on either side of the war. You three are scum. I wish I could just puke on what you have done."

Lawrence Brice thought he had him off guard at an emotional moment. He went for his right gun, arrogantly thinking a fast, single shot would do in the Widow Maker.

It had been months since Preacher had been forced to go one-on-one. His muscles and instinct were attuned to the

Whitworth. It nearly cost him his life. His senses had been on Brice's eyes and hands, but he had been thinking rifle. His draw was slow and off the mark. Brice was a lousy shot, but Preacher's first went wild over his shoulder. Luckily, Brice had drawn only on his first shot. Pumped up by his initial success, he now drew his second. Preacher was ready and angry. He was not ready to die, especially at the hands of this man. Before Brice got the second pistol out of leather, Preacher had cross drawn, aimed and fired.

Lawrence Brice had a moment of dream memory. He was back at West Point fighting a duel to the death. The adversary, with a sudden plunge, ran Brice through. That had been play acting. With a shudder, Larry Brice looked down to see that this wound was for true.

"You bastard!" James Brice shouted. "You've killed my father!"

"The man who was going to let you die by a firing squad," was the quiet answer.

"You lie!"

"Ask her. God, am I sick of war, and death, and people making me kill."

"Kill?" Betty Brice shrieked, near madness. "I am not ruined, you damn bastard! I will use every cent of Brice money to someday ruin you!"

James Brice remained silent, but vowed in his heart he would someday call out the gunslinger turned soldier.

Preacher took a chance for the first time in his life. He turned his back on the foe and walked away.

They could have gone for Brice's guns, but did not. He had figured they wouldn't. Betty Brice was too filled with personal grief and invictiveness. James Brice was too chicken. Later, Preacher knew he would have to fight each of them, on different battle fields. But, not on that day.

Preacher returned to the Raiders. It was time to bury the dead and care for the wounded. Brent's pen was not there to tell that story. Morgan Lake's heart could not endure it until years later.

The stop at Brice's Cross Landing was brief. Within a day, Forrest's Raiders were skirmishing for a new position in a war that did not wish to stop as a fighting machine.

PREACHER'S LAW

In the aftermath of the Civil War, Jeremy Preacher, late of Mosby's Rangers, rode home to find his plantation burned to the ground, his parents slaughtered and his sister brutally raped and murdered. Blood would flow, men would die and Preacher would be avenged—no matter how long it took. Join Preacher's bloody crusade for justice—from 1865 to 1908.

_____2588-4 #5: **Slaughter at Ten Sleep**
$2.75 US/$2.75 CAN

_____2576-0 #4: **The Last Gunfight**
$2.75 US/$3.75 CAN

_____2552-3 #3: **The Gavel and the Gun**
$2.75 US/$3.75 CAN

_____2528-0 #2: **Trail of Death**
$2.75 US/$3.75 CAN

_____2508-6 #1: **Widow Maker**
$2.75 US/$3.75 CAN

JIM STEEL MEANS GOLD, GUNS, WOMEN & BLOOD

The rip-roaring Western series that blasts off the page like a runaway train.

_____2485-3   #6:   AZTEC GOLD
                             $2.50 US/$3.25 CAN

_____2464-0   #5:   GOLD TRAIN
                             $2.50 US/$3.25 CAN

_____2440-3   #4:   DEVIL'S GOLD
                             $2.50 US/$3.25 CAN

_____2421-7   #3:   BLOODY GOLD
                             $2.50 US/$3.25 CAN

_____2399-7   #2:   DIE OF GOLD
                             $2.50 US/$3.25 CAN

PONY SOLDIERS

They were a dirty, undisciplined rabble, but they were the only chance a thousand settlers had to see another sunrise. Killing was their profession and they took pride in their work—they were too fierce to live, too damn mean to die.

_____2620-1   #5: SIOUX SHOWDOWN
                       $2.75 US/$3.75 CAN

_____2598-1   #4: CHEYENNE BLOOD STORM
                       $2.75US/$3.75CAN

_____2565-5   #3: COMANCHE MOON
                       $2.75US/$3.75CAN

_____2541-8   #2: COMANCHE MASSACRE
                       $2.75US/$3.75CAN

_____2518-3   #1: SLAUGHTER AT BUFFALO
                       CREEK $2.75US/$3.75CAN